THE SURFER

(SURFER TOWN I)

REBECCA CASTLE

ISBN: 9780645395907

PROLOGUE

LOVE IS A MYSTERIOUS FORCE.

You never know when or where it may cross your path in life.

And sometimes, when you least expect it...

Love finds you.

Even in the most unlikely of circumstances, love can find a way to cross your path.

Even when you're on the other side of the world, even when you don't think you deserve it.

Even when every thought in your head is pulling you away, your heart will tell you it is time.

Love can force you to see beyond the shallow façade someone's built up around themselves. It can help you strip away their layers like waves on sand, washing away their mask to see who they really are underneath.

Their true self.

It can help you see into their soul.

All you have to do is to be open to love whenever and wherever it chooses to find you.

And let it in.

1

COVE

Surfing is the best feeling in the entire world.

Yep.

Hands down.

It is beyond anything you can think of.

No joke.

I see you scoff, but really, *I ain't lying*.

Surfing is, by far, the best fucking thrill you can ever experience on this earth. Better than anything you can dream of. Go ahead, try me.

Anything.

Honestly - *and I mean this as a fucking fact* - I can put my hand over my heart and say that surfing is even better than girls.

There, I said it.

Girls.

As in sex. You know, the thing that a thousand songs have been sung about? That thing a thousand poems have been written for? Yeah. Surfing's better than that.

Really, it is better than any pussy you can find, and that's pretty big coming from me.

It's better than the most expensive alcoholic drinks you can buy in the most exclusive club. It's better than the best drugs you can score.

I bet you a hundred - no, a *million* - bucks that anyone who's spent a cool morning or a hot afternoon on a surfboard among the clear blue ocean waves will one hundred percent agree with me.

It's even better than the hottest and most mind-blowingly *rip-the-bedsheets-with-your-nails-awesome* sex you can imagine.

I've experienced that kind of sex *many* times before, and trust me, surfing beats it every day.

Surfing, in those glorious moments when the wind's blowing through your hair and you can smell the ocean salt whip off the wave behind you, is the best feeling in the entire world.

Truthfully.

And today, standing on my expensive surfboard knowing I'm just moments away from winning the biggest amateur surf competition in the Southern Hemisphere, is by far the best fucking day of my life.

I'm really feeling it.

And, right now, I am *loving* it.

On top of this surfboard, I am totally in my element. Standing on top of my board with my arms stretched out and my legs slightly bent, perfectly balanced, is completely natural to me.

Years of dedication have led me to this moment where I'm barreling down a massive wave at full speed in front of hundreds of spectators.

Years of endlessly waking up early to go to the beach for hard training are finally paying off in this very moment.

Years of carefully tracking my extreme diet have put me in the right athletic shape to pull this off. I mean, just take a look at my abs.

Years of abstention from drugs and girls and drink has made me one of the best amateur surfers in Australia.

The amount of fucking work and sacrifice I've put into this.

This trophy is guaranteed to be mine.

And now, at the Oceania Surf Competition, it's my chance to prove to the world that I really am ready.

This is my chance to prove to the world that I have been right all along. That I really am the best young male surfer in the Southern Hemisphere.

That I am a champion.

This win, basically guaranteed in a few moments time as long as I don't stuff it up, will be proof that I finally deserve to go pro. This will be enough proof that I deserve all the crazy fame and the glory that goes along with winning this coveted competition.

Right now, balancing on top of my surfboard, I can already see my future laid up before me, all the magazine covers, the interviews, the TV appearances, the golden trophies, the sick surfboards, the stunning girls.

The sponsorship deals.

The money.

The reputation.

I can picture them all so clearly.

They're practically mine already, as long as I don't fuck up.

And I won't fuck up. Not me. Not Cove Finn.

And, perhaps the most important of all to me, winning the Oceania Surf Competition will make my father proud. I know it will.

Forget about all the other crap; making my dad proud will be the most important prize of all.

And that's all that matters.

Beyond the girls and the fame and the massive lumps of cash, seeing my dad actually proud of me in the sport I've spent years carefully honing at will be the best thing to come out of today.

But don't get me wrong, I will *never* actually tell anyone else that my dad's pride will be the best thing to winning. Not in a million years will I dare admit that to anyone else. I'm definitely not some sentimental, emotional guy. I don't cry. I am not being all soppy.

I just know seeing my dad with a smile on his face when I hold that trophy up will make it all worth it.

And I am moments away from doing so.

Moments away from winning.

And I know it, I can *feel* it.

I am gonna win.

I'm riding down the biggest wave seen today at the competition. It's probably one of the biggest waves I've ever surfed in my life.

And it's all *mine*.

It's just me. Riding this monster wave. In front of a spectator stand full of people watching intensely. Years of training and paddling out to sea since I was a little boy have prepared me for this moment. And now all those years are paying off.

I am surfing.

And it's freaking amazing.

Like I've said, the best feeling in the entire world.

The best fucking feeling.

As I balance the board underneath my feet, I can see the beach not far away in front of me. I can see the hundreds of spectators gathered, watching with growing anticipation at what I'm about to accomplish here on this wave. If I pull this off correctly, I'll be the youngest surfer ever to win the Oceania Surf Competition since its inception in the seventies. I'm going to be a champion. The next Kelly Slater. The next world-famous surfer decorating the front pages of newspapers and surfing magazines for the next decade.

And I know that, standing on the beach in the spectator stand, will be my family. My older sister. My loving girlfriend.

My dad.

All there. They'll all be there in the stand, watching me as I come surfing down this wave at top speed. My body is perfectly toned, perfectly flexed for this challenge, perfectly balanced on my world-class surfboard performing moves I've practiced for years. My body's been fine-tuned to be a world-class surfing instrument. I have the muscles, and, most importantly, I have the Aussie beach boy's tan. I look the part. A real surfer's look.

I'm the real fucking deal.

And it's not just my family watching me on the beach; there's also professional surfing scouts, corporate sponsors, and famous surfers in the crowd today. They're the people I respect. They're the people I need to get on side if I'm to achieve my dream of being the best surfer in the world.

And this is my moment to prove to them I am capable of exactly that.

My girlfriend's in that crowd. My model - actually, *supermodel* – girlfriend. She's been on the front cover of every magazine in Australia, and at least half of the ones in America. She's a stunning piece of ass. I know she's there in the stands next to my older sister, observing me as I streak across this giant wave.

Man, if I win now, I'm gonna get the best blowjob tonight.

As my board smoothly cuts across the blue water of the wave, I can even hear the echoes of the PA system announcing me along the beach.

And here comes the young Cove Finn. It's his first time competing here, and he's only twenty years old. How about that?

Born in New Water, Cove comes from a business family in Australia. His father is the well-known business owner and CEO of Finn Companies. So, he's not just an attractive young surfer, but he's also the heir to a billionaire empire. Not too bad for a twenty-year-old. Let's see how he does here today and if he should win the most acclaimed prize in amateur surfing.

Can he do it?

Yeah, my dad's a billionaire owner of one of the biggest companies in Australia, but I never ever let that help or hinder my surfing chances. Ever since I was a boy, I've wanted to succeed in surfing on my own terms, not my father's. I never wanted my family's money to open up doors for me I can't manage on my own.

And Dad, despite his many doubts, reluctantly agreed to my requests for making it on my own back when I was just a kid. He allowed me to pursue this passion as long as it led to somewhere.

It was either surfing or business school, and I've always wanted to prove to him that I have what it takes within me to go the extra mile. That I have it in me to become the best surfer on planet earth.

And that's why, *right now*, I need to win.

I need to prove to him that he was right in trusting me. I need to prove to him that I am made to be a surfer.

I need to prove that this isn't just my passion.

I need to prove to him that this is my life's calling.

I look up from my surfboard to spot the spectator stand one more time, hoping to catch a glimpse of either my beautiful girlfriend or my sister.

Or even my dad watching me.

But looking up is a mistake.

A. Big. Mistake.

My legs tremble beneath me, my balance stumbles.

I've suddenly lost control of the board.

All those years of practice can't stop it from slipping away under my feet.

No.

All those years can't stop me from tumbling forward.

Shit.

And all those years can't stop me from falling, face forward, into the blue ocean at full speed. The impact's so strong it feels like my body's slamming into concrete.

Fuck.

And then the last thing I see before darkness takes over is the massive wave collapsing on top of me.

2

ONE YEAR LATER

COVE

THE GIRL in my bed smiles at me before she places her red lips around my cock. I lean back against my soft pillow and gently shut my eyes, enjoying the feel of her plump lips around my shaft.

Oh, man, I can already tell this is gonna be good.

I like it when they smile; those girls I lure back to my bed. I like to see the enjoyment in their eyes before they suck me off in the comfort of my own bedroom.

And this particular girl has a *great* fucking smile. All dazzling and perfectly shaped.

Just like her ass.

Her smile is even better than what I remember of it in the nightclub last night. Back then on the dancefloor, I was pretty much stoned out of my head to really register what she looked like or how nice her smile was in the darkness of the club, so it's pretty relieving in the morning light to see that I've somehow managed to take a real looker back home and not just some random ugly chick. It seems like last night I won the Russian roulette of pickup.

Thank God, even stoned me can pick the good ones out.

That's satisfying to know. I don't mind if she - and her gorgeous ass - stays wrapped up around my cock now that I've had a good look at her.

Thank God she's a solid ten-out-of-ten; I've been saved from an awkward conversation with an ugly girl trying to get her to leave. It's a conversation I've had to have far too many times in the past for me to admit.

And now it's morning, and I'm sober again, and this particular hot chick I've brought back from the club is going down on me just as I stir from slumber.

Very nice.

A girl pleasuring me in my own bed? What a beautiful way to wake up.

She gives off a small pleasurable moan as she manages to fit my whole cock into her inviting mouth. I reciprocate with one of my own moans. It's an impressive feat, managing to deep throat my dick, considering its size.

I like it when they smile, but I *especially* like it when they moan like the way she's currently doing. It's such a turn-on.

Yeah, what a truly beautiful way to wake up.

I open my eyes to catch another glimpse of her while she's preoccupied with teasing my cock. The first thing I notice is her long, flowing red hair. I'm not usually a fan of redheads, but this girl is a welcome exemption. It doesn't matter what color her hair is when she has those lips to die for and an hourglass body to match. Her hair's shade can be anything she wants it to be when she has a piece of ass like that.

With that kind of booty, she's my kind of woman.

And with what I can now remember of last night's antics in my bed, she's also a very *naughty* kind of woman.

Yep, exactly my type.

I think her name's Tessa. Or is it Toni? Taylor? Tegan? Something like that.

No. I'm sure it's Tessa. Her name definitely begins with T, I'm sure of it.

I'm sure she told me it's Tessa back in the club last night when we met on the dancefloor drunk and stoned out of our minds.

And now Tessa's doing something with her mouth that's making me squirm in orgasmic delight.

God, she's a natural.

From what I can feel, I think the trick has something to do with her tongue and how she's pressing it down on my cock. Somehow, she's using it to coax this enthusiastic reaction from me. I don't really care what the hell she's doing. Whatever it is, I hope she continues. I hope she doesn't stop.

I'm on the edge of climaxing any minute now.

Right on the *cusp...*

Fucking yes, this is definitely the perfect way to wake up.

My hands reach down and grab a handful of her silky red hair. She moans again at my touch and I feel my cock twitch in her mouth in response. Fuck me, she's *so* good.

I tug at her hair, rhythmically moving her head and, by extension, her mouth over and around my erect cock just the way I like it.

I like being in control.

She moans again. *Fuck.*

That's it. I can't take it anymore. This is it.

"I'm gonna cum," I breathlessly whisper. It's more a grunt than an actual articulated sentence.

Tessa unwraps her plump lips from my dick and instead

grabs it with both hands. I look at her, knowing I'm inches away from shooting my load. She smiles again, her fucking *great* smile.

That's enough to send me over the edge.

"Go ahead, big boy," she teases.

Yeah, more than enough to send me over the edge.

My cock unloads onto her exposed, perky breasts. Tessa watches me as I close my eyes again and moan once more.

Yeah, what a fucking nice way to wake up.

Completely spent, I relax for a moment on my bed. My body's loose. I can't feel my limbs. I sigh and I blink open my eyes to see that Tessa's still here, smiling at me.

"How's that?" she asks, murmuring delicately. "Was it good?"

"Yeah." It's all I can manage as a response. I don't have the energy to talk to her. Girls always want to check up on you straight after you cum, to make sure you're okay just at the *precise* moment you want to chill the fuck out.

Just leave me the fuck alone now. You've done your job.

The mattress shakes under me as Tessa stands up on my bed. I get to see her whole body now. She must've picked up one of my shirts because she's wearing one now. And just her black panties. Her long slender legs fit perfectly onto her nice, round ass. I can see her tits poking invitingly through my shirt. She's model material all right. What a stunner. And now she's headed straight back to me.

She continues smiling at me as she lies down on the pillow next to my relaxed body. But the moment I feel the warmth from her skin touch mine, I immediately push myself out of bed. I need to get up and away from her.

None of this touchy-feely post-sex crap, please.

I stand, completely naked, in the middle of my bedroom. This house is technically my sister's. Sandy. I'm sharing it with her and have been ever since I got back from the hospital after the... accident.

I search around the room. It's pretty messy in here.

Alright, it's *super* messy.

It's like a bomb's gone off and has blown everything I own around the place. My room's a complete and utter pigsty. Dirty laundry lies scattered everywhere. Random things from my past are placed sporadically on every shelf and table surface. Photo frames. Important documents. Books I haven't read. There's no order to anything inside my man cave. You can't see the floor through the clothes I've thrown down and accumulated over the months I've lived here. My sister absolutely hates it.

Bending over in the middle of my room, I pick up an item, an old dirty shirt of mine, and use that to clean my naked body from the blowjob's mess. All done, I aim the shirt at the trash can in the corner. I shoot. *BANG*. Score. The shirt's in the bin. Even I wouldn't leave that shirt lying around anymore, not with the remnants of the glorious blowjob I've just had now staining it.

I take a step back towards the bed and nearly slip on an old sock under my foot.

Ouch.

Look, I don't care about my room or how messy it is. I don't care what I must seem like to anyone who comes in here, and I certainly don't care what my sister thinks of my lifestyle.

To be honest, I don't really care much about anything at all.

And I especially don't care about the girl in my bed. She's now properly lying there, snuggling up against the spot where I was just relaxing moments earlier, savoring the sheets warmed by my muscular male body.

She looks at me from under her long eyelashes and practically *purrs*, inviting me back to bed with her expectant expression.

"Let's cuddle," she says with her sultry voice. She's trying so hard.

Why the fuck do girls love cuddling after sex?

Why are they so goddamn needy all the time?

Can't she see me for who I am? See my muscles? I'm definitely not the cuddling type. Can't she see I am not worth the effort?

Can't she see that, deep down, she wouldn't even want me?

If she really knew me, she wouldn't.

No one in their right mind should want me and my failed ass.

She's still staring at my eyes and I suddenly have an urge to look away, to not meet her penetrating focus.

I avert my face down to the ground and catch sight of my naked body, especially my legs. And not just my legs, but the two long scars running up each one, both a stark reminder of the surgeries I've received in the last year. A reminder of the long days in the hospital. That painful time spent recovering from the accident at the Oceania Surf Competition.

It'd been one year since that fateful day when everything good in my life ended and when I gave up caring about anything.

One year since my dreams fell to pieces in a raging ball of fire.

One year of excruciating pain and endless torture just to get out of the fucking hospital bed.

And now, one year on, all I do is drink, get high, and fuck the brains out of eager girls like this Tessa currently occupying my bed.

Looking down at these two scars running down my legs

makes me angry, and it also makes me ask the question in my mind again.

Can't she see that she doesn't want me?

No one in their right mind would, especially knowing who I am and who I've become. Those long scars are proof enough.

I'm nothing but a failure.

"I'm not going to bed, Tessa," I reply to her flatly. I want to get out of here, out of my room, and away from her. I don't want to see her flirtatious looks inviting me to cuddle. I suddenly and desperately want to be on my own and away from everybody else in the entire world.

"Oh?"

I need an excuse to get out. To escape from this new nightmare.

"I'm going to get a joint from the kitchen."

Hey, it's a shit excuse, but at least it's something.

There's a pause.

"Tanya."

"What?" I ask.

"It's Tanya," she replies softly. "My name's not Tessa. It's Tanya. I told you that last night, and in the taxi back here, and about five minutes ago when we woke up."

Oh. Right.

Fuck.

Well, I did think it started with T, so I am *kinda* right in a way. I was completely fucked out of my head the night before, okay? Why should I remember some random girl's name?

Look, I should be congratulated for even knowing it started with T.

Fuck it.

I don't reply to her correction. Instead, I stroll, still naked, over to the pile of dirty clothes that constitute my bedroom floor and open the door into the open-plan living room and kitchen of my sister's house. I know Sandy's at work as a teacher, so there's no one else in the house to catch me naked. I just need to get out of this bedroom and away from Tessa - *Tanya*. Whatever it is she's calling herself.

I step out into the spacious living room and kitchen area, closing my bedroom door behind me. My long, thick cock sways proudly between my legs and I gladly feel the morning breeze against it.

Maybe in a moment Tanya might forget about the little name slip-up and let me go for round two.

But something is wrong. My senses are tingling like I'm being watched.

I look up.

I am being watched.

Oh, fuck.

Standing in the middle of the living room is Sandy.

And right next to my sister is a stranger. A strange girl I have never seen before.

I am standing outside my bedroom door, completely and utterly naked, with my sister and a strange geeky girl staring right back at me.

Who the fuck's this?

And this is when I meet *her*.

The girl who will ruin my life.

3

TWO HOURS EARLIER

RIPLEY

"So, why are you attempting to enter Australia, Miss Ripley Sailor?"

The border guard takes one quick look at my passport photo and then back up to me. Back up to my face. I attempt a sweet smile to cool his tone, but he's staring at me with dark cold eyes that dig deep into my soul.

Yep. My smile isn't working. The man's not budging.

It is definitely *not* the question I'm hoping to be faced with after traveling so long in the air around the world.

And the border guard's bark when he asks it doesn't make the question any more pleasant.

"Why are you attempting to enter Australia, Miss Sailor?"

He questions me like I'm some kind of criminal. This is less of a polite check at the border and more like a military-style interrogation. He's treating me like I'm some kind of evil mastermind trying to trick him in order to enter his country illegally and cause trouble, and he's the only protection standing in my way. He must think he's some tough cop like Bruce Willis from *Die Hard*.

But me? All I want is a shower. A nice warm shower.

And maybe a bar of soap.

I just don't want to smell so bad; that's all I'm asking for.

"What?" I'm so stressed out and tired from flying halfway around the globe that this is all I can muster up to the border guard in reply. Monosyllabic, I know, but all I'm thinking of is that hot stream of water finally hitting my back.

The border guard doesn't seem very impressed with my reply. He sighs.

A deep, long sigh.

This is not good.

I know I should be more responsive and attentive to the border guard's questions, but I just can't stop staring at his mustache. A perfectly groomed handlebar mustache that's plastered thickly over his thin mouth. I can't decide whether he looks more like a street thug or a porn star from the seventies.

I don't have the energy required for this sudden pressure. I've been waiting in this line a long time, gripping my tattered American passport like my life depends on it. Well, maybe not my life, but at least the chance for that nice warm shower I'm dreaming of.

And when it is finally my turn to step up to the scary-looking border gate with all the security cameras dotted around and the imposing mustached guard's barking tone, my mind just completely blanks out on me. I'm tired, sore, and in urgent need of a wash. I can't even think, and I can't answer questions, let alone questions from a man with such a thick handlebar mustache.

Yep, on closer inspection, I think it's closer to 70s porn star.

"What is the meaning of your visit to Australia? Why did you decide to leave New York to come here?"

My eyes quickly dart down to the name tag pinned on the man's navy-blue uniform right next to the flag of Australia.

GARY.

Yeah, somehow, he looks like a Gary. Not that I'm judging him or anything, and not that Gary is a particularly *odd* name at all. But this guy is just, somehow, giving off some strong... *Gary vibes*.

"It's kind of a long story," I say. I try smiling again, but Gary the border guard is having none of it.

"Enlighten me."

"Well, it's a bit complicated, but essentially, I'm here to look after a friend's brother." I chuckle. "It sounds a bit weird putting it like that."

Somehow, Gary frowns even further, sending his mustache into an angry droop. I can see my answer has not helped the situation. "So, you're staying with a friend?" he asks.

"Yeah."

"And have you met this friend before?"

"Yeah. Well, no," I reply, and Gary raises his eyebrow. His mustache twitches. "Not exactly. Not physically, but we've met online."

"Online?"

"We're internet friends. You know, the modern world," I explain, unhelpfully throwing my hands up in the air to indicate the internet traveling all around us. I hope this answer would be enough to satisfy Gary, but by the look on his face, I realize I've only made things worse.

Whoops.

But I am telling the truth. Sandy and I are *really* good friends, except for the small fact we've never actually met in real life.

Sure, we've Skyped and Facetimed and everything else you can do when you're separated by multiple oceans, but it isn't the same as seeing each other face to face.

Which we're trying to do. If Gary will let me past the border.

Sandy and I met online nearly a year ago over our shared love of *The Vindicator Team*, the big superhero film franchise that dominates the box office charts. We met on an internet forum for the film series, a forum where angry men discuss minute details about every facet of the film series. It seemed like we are the only girls on the site, surrounded by these intense male commentators, so we just have no choice but to bond. We bonded over our shared love of the film franchise and we continued chatting on our own social media, away from the angry male comments found on the internet forums. We basically became instant friends from the moment we found each other on that site, and we've talked every day from then on.

Our conversations quickly moved on from *The Vindicator Team* and into our daily lives. We know everything about each other, more than any other friend I've ever had.

I think it's pretty safe to say that Sandy is my best friend.

We just haven't met in *real* life, that's all.

But I don't think Gary the border guard is completely understanding on that point. I wonder - by the way he's staring at me with seething resentment - if he's even heard of the internet. I have to bite my tongue and not try to patronizingly explain what the internet is to him. Somehow, I don't think he'll appreciate that.

I know Sandy is real and not some kind of catfish, but she lives all the way over in a small surfer town in Australia and I live in a small apartment in Queens, New York.

We're pretty far apart. Worlds apart, even.

But somehow, we became friends super easily over the internet, and now I'm here. At the Australian border gate at New Water Airport about to meet my best friend for the first time *in person*.

I know Sandy will be waiting for me in the Arrivals Lounge just a few dozen yards away beyond the gate. All that stands between me and her and I properly meeting for the first time is a thick handlebar mustache.

And I know that mustache is not letting me go anywhere anytime soon.

"Internet friends?" Gary repeats, glancing back at my passport. I follow his eyes down to my dreaded passport photo and I gulp. I know what he's looking at. My passport photo isn't the best photo of me, that's for sure. It doesn't even look like me anymore.

The thing was taken three years ago, back when I was seventeen and in the thralls of the worst time in my teenage life. Acne. Dry skin. Greasy hair. Yep, my passport photo is proud to display all the worst facets of being a geeky teenage girl.

And now Gary, the border guard, is studying it like it's the first photo that pops up on the FBI's Most Wanted List. Well, at least I've grown out of that awkward teenage phase and I'm no longer covered in spots and bad skin.

I'm twenty now. Brown eyes. Brown, shoulder-length wavy hair. Pale skin. Just your typical girl from Queens and not a world-class terrorist.

If only Gary can see that.

This trip - if I even make it out of the airport - is going to be my first time in Australia. In fact, it's going to be my first ever time out of America. I've had to board three long-ass flights to even get here to New Water. New York to LA, then LA to Sydney, and then finally Sydney to New Water. I've practically spent *days* in the air. Days without sight of a single shower or a bar of soap.

I bet there is a high chance that Gary can smell me even through the big glass window separating him from me, and I bet that also doesn't help my case.

"You're looking after her brother?" he asks, eyeing the passport photo.

Great.

Okay, I'm going to have to explain more about the strange situation I've found myself in. I take a deep breath to clear my cloudy, jetlagged mind, readying myself for another one of my infamous long-winded rambles.

Think, Ripley, think. Communicate this correctly.

"Yeah, it's kind of a nursing thing," I reply. "I'm a nurse, well, not exactly. I'm about to study nursing at university back home, so I'm not a nurse just yet. I'm a student. Well, not even technically a student, because I haven't even started yet. But, yeah, I'm a nursing student."

God, I talk so much when I'm nervous.

"Right." Gary's tone is deadpan and unmoving. Call me a psychic, but I'm starting to really get the sense that Gary is really, really unimpressed by my answers. It's just a teeny tiny little hunch I have that this is not going well at all.

I'm going to be kicked out of Australia before I've even properly taken a step into the airport's Arrivals Lounge.

"Yeah. Like I said, it's a long story."

"I see. And who is this friend of yours?"

"Her name's Sandy," I reply. It's the one answer I can give that can make any sense. "Sandy Finn."

Gary's eyes widen at the name. "Sandy Finn?" he stutters. "As in *Finn*?"

"Yep."

"And her brother is Cove Finn?"

So, he knows them? "Yeah, that's it," I reply, shrugging.

"You're staying with a Finn?"

"Apparently, both her *and* her brother, actually. Two Finns."

Gary pauses for a moment. His veneer of a professional *take-no-bullshit* interrogator disappears, and a certain look comes over his face. I recognize that expression immediately.

It's a look of fear.

Wow.

Something's made Gary change so quickly.

Was it Sandy's name?

He hastily stamps my passport and hands it back to me without a word.

I can't help but notice his hand shaking.

But I'm being let into the country, and that's all that counts, right?

"Thanks," I say, surprised at this sudden turn of events.

"Go on through," Gary replies, quickly waving me through the border control barriers. He's staring at his computer screen, refusing to even look me in the eye. Or maybe he's too scared to. "Welcome to Australia."

I don't believe my luck. All I have to do is mention Sandy's name and this government official simply just *waves* me through border control into his country, despite his suspicions?

What have I gotten myself into here?

But I don't question him. Despite my jetlagged ramblings, I'm smart enough not to. I simply pick up my travel bag and stroll right on through the border gate, heading straight towards the Arrival Lounge.

Straight through to Sandy.

I mean, I know her family is rich and famous and can open the right doors with the right people, but I didn't know that just the mere mention of Sandy's last name would actually *physically* open the doors at border control.

My best friend's family is probably tied up in some pretty heavy illegal shit.

And now I'm going to be staying with her and her brother for a very, very long time. Two people I haven't even properly met yet.

I step into the Arrivals Lounge, holding my breath.

Well, at least I made it through the border.

So. Here goes.

Australia.

4

RIPLEY

THE FIRST THING I see when I step through the gate into the Arrivals Lounge is the massive Kangaroo stuffed toy.

And the next thing I see is the equally massive sign announcing my name in large handwritten block letters.

WELCOME TO AUSTRALIA RIPLEY SAILOR.

Of course.

Sandy.

My best friend's waiting for me, leaning over the airport barrier with the biggest smile on her face, the handwritten sign in one hand and the giant stuffed kangaroo in the other. I recognize her immediately even though we've never met in person; she just looks exactly like I imagine. She's told me online how she's a tall girl, but I'm still surprised by her five-foot-eight height. I'm tiny compared to her.

She looks like a goddamn *supermodel.*

Slim. Tanned. Long blonde hair.

Wow.

I mean, I'm not too surprised by her overwhelming

beauty. She never looks anything but immaculate on all our Facetime calls with each other, but it's pretty blinding actually seeing her in the flesh right here in front of me in the airport.

It's definitely, without a doubt, *her*.

My heart stops. I can't believe I've made it here; even after all the long tiring flights and severe lack of soap, I'm still so absolutely excited seeing my best friend in person. I want to do a little dance right now in the airport, even with everyone watching, and I'm a pretty shy girl. I just can't believe it. I'm *here*, standing in front of Sandy.

In Australia.

Sandy squeals in excitement and lifts her arms over the barrier. I don't need an invite; I rush into her arms, enveloped by the biggest hug from her. A well-deserved hug after all those cramped hours sitting in the air.

I've made it.

The waist-high barrier is caught between us, but it doesn't matter. Our arms fit perfectly around each other.

"Sandy!"

"Ripley!"

I've been super nervous on the flight over whether our chemistry will survive meeting in person, but these first few moments in the airport Arrival Lounge entirely dispel any anxiety I have left. We are like sisters greeting each other. Sandy is a few years older than me, at twenty-four, and I've just turned twenty a few months ago, so she is kinda like my older sister.

Sandy lets go of me and I drop my bag.

"I can't believe you're here," she says, motioning me around the barrier. She leaves the giant stuffed kangaroo toy on the airport ground and hugs me again.

"I'm so happy I've made it," I reply into her hair as she squeezes me tight.

"I've had to wait ages," Sandy says, letting me go from her embrace. "The incoming flights board said your plane landed ages ago. What kept you so long? Are you okay?"

I gesture back towards the border gate. "The border guards are *very* thorough," I reply. "Let's get a selfie. My Mom was non-stop pestering me about getting one with you for weeks before I left."

It's true, all my Mom wants is a photo of Sandy and me together at the airport. Sandy leans in over my shoulder as I snap us on my phone.

Mom.

I miss her already. My mind drifts back to the apartment we share back home in Queens and how lonely she must be feeling stuck there now. Mom and I have never spent more than a few days apart ever since the day I was born. This trip away from her will be a big thing for her.

It'd be a big thing for me.

Photo taken, Sandy winks and leans over to pick up my bag, leaving me to hold the giant stuffed kangaroo. "I can't stand it in here anymore," she says. "Let's get to the car. I'm sure you're aching for a shower."

I shrug, resisting the temptation to smell my armpits. "Oh, more than you'd believe, Sandy. More than you'd believe."

* * *

Sandy's car is SUPER, *super* nice.

Look, I'm not a car girl. I can barely even drive or tell you the difference between a Ferrari or a Lamborghini, but even I can tell that this is one nice ride. It's some kind of sports car. Tinted windows, shiny exterior, dark leather seats. The whole lot.

Super, super nice.

"Fancy," I remark upon seeing it stationed at the top level of the airport parking lot.

Sandy rolls her eyes at my comment, embarrassed. "Yeah, it's nicer than a normal car on a teacher's salary, but that's only because dad really, really wanted to give it to me as a gift for my birthday."

I nod. "Right."

Don't forget how crazy rich their family is. Or how the mere mention of their name can open up the border.

"I'm against taking money from dad, but he insisted. He told me that no child of his is driving around in a shit car. They are his exact words, and you can't change his mind once he's made a decision."

To be honest, I'm kinda glad Sandy's the first one to mention money. With her family being one of the richest families in Australia, probably the richest in her state, I've always felt super weird ever mentioning money in our conversations, even in passing. We've never really spoken about her family's wealth at all, and I never want to raise it. Sandy's my best friend and what money she has or doesn't have is really none of my concern. I'm sure she and her dad have enough people forcing themselves into their lives just for a quick buck as it is without me making it an issue wedging between us as friends. That isn't me. That's not what I'm doing by being Sandy's friend. That isn't who I'm.

And what I admire about Sandy is that she isn't like that at all either. She doesn't live off her dad's empire. Instead, she made her own way in the world. She works as a teacher at the local private school, paying for her own way in life. She's paid for everything she owned, except for this car. She's independent, even despite her dad's efforts to lavish her with an inheritance.

And that's another reason why she's my best friend.

She unlocks the car, pushing my bag onto the back seat.

We somehow manage to shove in the giant kangaroo and then we jump into the front. Sandy turns on the ignition and we zoom out of there, out of the airport parking lot, and onto the highway.

Australia.

I stare out the window as we speed down the highway in Sandy's fast sports car. I've never been to another country before. I just look out the car window in awe at the foreign countryside shooting past.

I've seen films about Australia and have always thought it beautiful, but actually seeing it with my own eyes is breathtaking.

New Water, Sandy's hometown, is, as its name suggests, situated right next to the ocean. It's just what you imagine of a postcard-ready snapshot of an Australian beach town. Lots of white houses nestled between gum trees. Long sandy beaches barely touched. Rolling hills on the horizon. Picture perfect.

Better take a photo and send it to Mom. She'll love this.

With my face pressing hard against the window, I take it all in. It doesn't matter how stressed and tired and dirty I am from the endless flights; the countryside is just so damn *beautiful*.

I can't believe I'm really here.

This is a long way from the small cramped apartment I share with my Mom in Queens. This is a long way from the skyscrapers and tightly packed urban landscape back home.

As I stare out the car window, I feel Sandy's hand on my knee. I turn back around to see her smiling at me, her other hand on the steering wheel. "I'm so glad you've come," she says. "I'm so glad you've decided to do this with my brother."

Ah. So, we're already talking about Cove then?

Here we go.

"I'm pretty taken aback when you first asked me about it," I reply.

"I know. It's a big ask, especially with Cove. But I'm glad you've come," Sandy says. "Are you sure you're okay doing this? You still don't have to if you don't want."

I look at her stunning blue eyes. She looks just like a typical Aussie surfer girl you'd see in one of their famous drama soaps. Beautiful, blonde, and tanned. She could be related to a Hemsworth. "You're crazy? I'm here. I'm happy to do this," I reply.

"It's not weird or anything?"

A little weird.

"Well, as I say, it did take me a while to come around to the idea. But I'm here now, aren't I? I've made the trip."

Cove, Sandy's brother, is the real reason for my trip. Sandy first spoke to me about her younger brother a few months back, telling me the story behind the last year of his life. The surfing accident. The scars on his legs. The fact he's given up on everything good in his life and has moved into her place to just laze around all day by smoking weed and drinking.

He sounds like a real charmer.

"Okay. You can always talk to me, though. If you want," Sandy says, changing lanes on the highway. "I'm always here for you."

I smile back at my best friend. "I know."

"Trust me, it'll be worth your while. You won't regret coming here, we need you. A lot."

"It's that bad, huh?"

Sandy sighs. "Yeah, it's that bad. Cove's had a hard time, but now he's just sulking around like a petulant child and it's just infuriating. I'm at my wit's end. The very end."

"Why? What's happened?"

"Well, for starters, there's a different girl every night in his room."

"What? Like, every night?"

"Yeah."

"Doesn't he have a girlfriend or something?"

"He did, and she's *insanely* beautiful. A world-famous supermodel. But she left him once he had the surfing accident. She just sent him a breakup text when he was still in hospital just waking up from surgery, like, literally as he was waking up. It was perfectly timed to inflict the most emotional damage on him and, yeah, he took that pretty hard."

"I'd bet. Wow, that's cruel."

Sandy turns to me and shakes her head. "But don't you dare start feeling sorry for him. He's not some lost puppy to pet and fawn over. He knows exactly what he's doing, and he knows the consequences. I've given him enough chances; *our* dad has given him enough chances. This is it for him, the end of the line."

I've never seen Sandy so riled up; her brother really has taken her to her tipping point. "His accident was a year ago, right?"

"Yeah, the Oceania Surfing Competition, that was when he fell off his board, lost the competition, and messed up his legs."

"One year and he's still recovering?"

"*Recovering?*" Sandy tuts under her breath, her sarcasm practically dripping. "There's no need for him to physically recover anymore. He's one hundred percent fine now. The only thing that needs recovering is his attitude. Wait, it doesn't need recovering, it needs *fixing*."

"Well, hopefully, I can help."

Sandy turns away from me and back to the window

with both her hands tightly gripped around the steering wheel. "Hopefully you can."

Oh, so Cove is worse than I've thought if he's winding Sandy up like this. *Way worse.*

A different girl in his bed every night? Sulking around? Not surfing anymore? Drink and drugs?

I know exactly who Cove Finn is.

A *bad boy*.

A player. A classic scoundrel.

And Sandy thinks that, somehow, I'll be the one to come over here and fix him?

Good luck to me.

Well, let me meet him first and then we'll see.

He can't honestly be *that* bad. Not as bad as Sandy is making him out to be, surely?

I sink back in the leather car seat and rub my jetlagged forehead. The first thing I need to do before meeting Cove, or any other bad boys for that matter, will be a shower. *ASAP.*

We continue off the highway and onto a long winding road heading down towards New Water. I can see the whole town now in all its glory. The beaches. The surf.

I can even see an array of little dots far out in the ocean. It takes me a moment to realize what they are. Surfers. Sitting on their surfboards, ready for the next wave to take them to shore.

It's early morning. The sun is rising. The surfers are enjoying the first rays of sunshine.

This town really is paradise.

And then I can see them, more dark shapes beyond the surfers, even further out in the sea. Shapes that are moving fast, jumping in and out of the clear blue water.

No, they can't be.

"Are those dolphins?" I ask Sandy in disbelief, pointing

my finger against the car's window towards the fast, black dots in the ocean below. Sandy quickly glances over as to not take her eyes off the road for too long. She doesn't seem nearly as amazed as I'm to be seeing what I'm seeing.

"Yeah, they are," she says matter-of-factly. "They sometimes like to swim near the surfers."

I pressed my face against the window. "This is insane," I whisper in shock. I've never seen dolphins in the wild before, only at the aquarium in downtown New York.

This is a totally different world.

Sandy smiled at me and again places her hand back on my knee.

"Thank you again for coming here," she says.

I truly am happy to be here, but the words about her brother are still stuck in a loop in my head.

A bad boy.

And I'm the one somehow expected to fix him.

That's the reason for this trip.

As I watch the dolphins dance in the ocean, I can't help but think about this Cove dude I haven't met yet, and what I've gotten myself into by coming to this country.

Well, it's too late to turn back now; I'm about to meet the bastard.

5

RIPLEY

"WE'RE HERE," Sandy says as she turns the steering wheel of her sports car.

And that's it. With a squeak of the car's tires, we pull into the driveway leading up to Sandy's house.

I don't want to repeat myself like I've done about all my observations about Australia, but her house is an *amazing* place. Another amazing place in this amazing country. Painted white on the outside, the house has large glass windows that let you see into the large living space. The place is big, like all the houses we passed by in New Water are. Situated amongst palm trees, Sandy's house is isolated from its neighbors by the thick bushland surrounding it. Standing outside the long building, you really felt you are in the country and yet you are not far from the town.

This is tropical heaven.

Inside's no different from the isolated beauty outside. Inside, the house is spacious and open-planned in a modern style. Tall glass windows on the other side of the house look out over the ocean. You can *actually* see the clear blue water of the Pacific Ocean directly from the counter in Sandy's kitchen.

Yet again, repeating myself, it's *amazing*.

The house takes my breath away when I step through the front door and see the view from inside with the giant stuffed kangaroo toy jammed under my arm. Sandy follows me inside, holding my travel bag with both hands. She grins at me with her white teeth as I stare in awe at her home.

"This place is perfect," I utter, looking around the kitchen and living space and shaking my head.

Yeah, this is a long way from the small apartment I share with Mom back in Queens.

"Welcome to my place," Sandy replies, placing my bag next to the kitchen counter. Hands free, she has the chance to gesture around the house and to show me the details. "Your room is over there, next to Cove's. There's an en-suite in there as well, so you don't have to worry about sharing a shower stall with a dirty boy." She points at a room next to the front door. Cove's room.

He's directly next to mine.

The door to his room is shut.

Imposing.

"Is Cove in now?" I ask, biting my lip nervously.

"Probably. He's either in there or he's collapsed outside the nightclub in town. It's still morning, so he'll be fast asleep no matter where he is in the world," Sandy says, sighing. "My room is at the back of the house, and, as you can see, this is the kitchen-slash-living room. Make yourself at home. What's mine is yours."

"Thanks, Sandy."

"As I keep saying, it's good to have you here."

This time I sniff my armpits. *Oh, God.* "I need a shower," I say, and Sandy laughs. I guess she must've been able to smell me the entire trip here from the airport, especially in the confines of her car.

Great first impression, Ripley. Just great.

And then Cove's door behind me flies open and Sandy's brother walks out, slamming the door behind him. We notice him before he notices us. He doesn't even know we're here.

It's him.

Sandy and I stand completely still, like statues, as we stare at him. We're shocked at what we are seeing. shocked at what he's wearing.

Or, actually, shocked at more of what he isn't wearing.

Cove is completely and utterly naked.

Oh my god.

He looks up at us, confused by our expressions as we stare at him.

"What?" he asks.

He doesn't know.

"Cove," Sandy spluttered at her younger brother. "You're naked."

He slowly looks down at his exposed, swaying cock and then back up at us. He smiles a broad cocky smile, realizing the situation at last.

"So, it appears I am," he replies without a care in the world.

I can't believe him. He's *smirking*. He's naked and the first thing he thought to do is *smirk* at us?

What's going on? Who is this guy to not care he's naked in front of his sister and a stranger?

I can't move. I'm so surprised at what I'm seeing. Cove's exposed body. It's the last thing I've expected to come across on a bright early Australian morning after days of flying across the globe.

Especially Cove's dick swinging between his legs.

I've never seen a cock so thick and long in all my life. The thing is *massive*.

No wonder Cove has a big ego when he has such a... big... member.

And Cove follows his older sister in the looks department. She's stunning, but, my God, he's absolutely *gorgeous*. And now he's standing, completely naked, in front of me. I can see everything.

Everything.

No wonder he's able to score a new girl every night when he has a body like that. He has that typical laid-back Aussie surfer look. His wavy bleach-blonde hair is messed to fuckable perfection, his skin is tanned from days in the sun and years spent in the salty ocean, his body is built like a Greek statue, all athleticism, and toned curves. The sharp shape of his jawline is to die for. His abs are defined and popped out; all I want to do is touch them. Feel their solid shape with my own hands. His biceps ripple with every movement of his arms. His legs are slender and muscular.

The sight of his perfect body does things to mine that I haven't felt for a long time. Something stirs within me.

No, Ripley.

Remember what Sandy described him as. Who he is. What he does.

He's a bad guy, but he's everything you think of when you think of a muscular Aussie surfer boy. Completely and totally irresistible to a geeky girl from Queens.

And, best of all, his eyes are a piercing blue that makes my heart flutter when he looks at me.

And he *is* looking at me.

He's staring at me with a penetrating glare. He isn't interested in his sister at all.

He's interested in *me*.

"And why the fuck are you naked, Cove?" Sandy asks, her voice becoming more and more incredulous with every word she utters. She's using her proper big-sister voice.

Cove shrugs. "I thought you are at work, sis. Not my fault you're seeing me like this. You know I don't really care about clothes at the best of times."

He should've been looking at Sandy, but all his attention remains on me.

His bright blue eyes *remain* on me.

His accent fills my ears like golden syrup, and I can just lose myself in his broad voice. A rough, strong, deep Aussie accent that I feel resonating through my chest.

My body shudders. Yeah, he's definitely attractive alright, but I can see he's trouble. *Real* trouble. The dangerous kind. The kind I shouldn't be involved in.

The alarm bells in my mind are triggering, telling me that he's dangerous and not to be played with. I know I'll only get burned.

I see his legs and the long scars on each one. I know immediately they are the ones from his surfing accident. The accident that led to him losing his lifestyle, the accident that led him to not surf again, that led to his breakup, that led to him lazing around town, getting high and fucking the nearest pussy.

The accident that led to me being in this house right here, right now.

"And you think just because you thought I'm at work gives you the right to walk around completely naked?" Sandy snidely replies to her brother. "Get some clothes on. We have a guest."

Cove waves his hand towards me. "And who's she?" he asks, still not breaking eye contact with me.

Rude.

Sandy also seems irritated by his arrogant question.

"This is my best friend, Ripley Sailor. I've told you about her and how she's staying with us for the next few months, if you even remember."

I don't like being talked about as if I'm not in the room, so I offer my hand out to the surfer boy for a handshake.

"I'm Ripley," I say. "Nice to meet you, Cove."

He doesn't bother retreating into his room to put on some clothes before he introduces himself. Instead, he takes a few steps forward so that we are so close our faces can touch if I lean just slightly forward. We are so close I can see the drops of sweat on his neck. We're so close I can take in his smell, a pure, natural manly scent. Somehow, I can sense he's just had sex; he has that fresh, warm lazy vibe around him. I can tell he's just had sex and has *really* enjoyed it. That makes me shiver with trepidation. Here's a man who gets what he wants. His body is so warm I can feel it from where I am. He's a great big muscular hunk standing over me. He's completely naked in front of some strange girl and he doesn't care one bit.

This is some kind of power play.

Who the fuck is this guy?

I try to maintain eye contact and *not* divert my attention down to the massive cock hanging between his legs. It's pretty tempting to do, but I remain composed. I really want another sneak peek at the cock, though. He's pretty irresistible.

No, stop it.

I'm going to be cool and collected. I'm not going to give him the satisfaction of acknowledging his immense member. I have the sneaking suspicion he'd like it if I do.

Standing so close that we are nearly touching, Cove takes a quick glance at my outstretched hand and then back at me.

His full, kissable lips curl in a sneer as he takes me in. He scans my body up and down with his bright blue eyes.

He doesn't shake my hand.

"Hello, Ripley," he whispers. I feel like it's a threat somehow. Like he's trying to intimidate me. And, yeah, it's working. "You're American?"

I'm uncomfortable with his close proximity, but I decide to hide it. No way am I gonna let this arrogant dick with the massive dick sense any kind of weakness in me; I'm gonna fight fire with fire.

"I am American," I reply forcefully. "You have a problem with that?"

"Depends on how much of a problem you are."

"I'm not a problem," I stutter, his strong gaze unnerving me. Cove chuckles quietly.

What an asshole.

"So, she's your new spy on me, then?" he asks his sister, still glaring at me with his piercing eyes. God, I'm melting under his glare, both in anger and desire. "She's interesting, this American girl."

Wait, hold on.

American girl?

Is that all I am to him? Some Yank? Some stupid American?

The way he says it, the way he savors the words. He's trying to play with my head. He wants to bully me. He wants to make me feel small.

Good luck with that, Cove Finn.

I really, really hate being talked about as if I'm not standing right there nearly touching his thick cock.

"Cove! Come back to bed!"

The voice comes from within Cove's room. A female voice.

Cove rolls his eyes at the mention of his name.

There's a girl in his bed? Right now?

"Who's this one, then?" Sandy asks, her arms crossed. Judging from her nonchalant reaction, this is clearly a daily occurrence in their household.

"I can't remember," Cove replies, casually scratching the back of his bleach-blonde hair. "I do think her name starts with T, though."

"Well, that's a whole lot more knowledge than you have of the girl in your bed yesterday."

"Cove!" the girl in the bedroom seductively calls out again, the voice echoing through the open-plan house and into the wide kitchen where we're standing.

A girl is currently in his bed and Cove's standing stark naked in front of us. This is *definitely* not how I'm expecting my first morning in Australia to go.

And I still urgently need that shower.

"I should go. My horde of adoring fans needs me," Cove says. He sneers at me again. "Nice to meet you, Ripley Sailor. In my opinion, it'll be best for you to just jump on the next plane back to wherever in America you came from. I would say *see you around*, but hopefully, I don't."

And with that snide remark, he turns around and heads straight back into his room, slamming his door shut behind him, giving me a clear view of his ripped back and his tight, muscular ass. I also get a clear view of the small dolphin-shaped tattoo sitting in the middle of his lower back.

A dolphin tattoo? Strange.

And then he's gone.

I stand completely still, amazed by our brief encounter. He's like a gust of forceful wind, and he very nearly blew me over. I don't know whether to hate him for what he's said to me or fancy his toned, irresistible body. I explain my lust away for being the wild thoughts of a jetlagged mind.

You're being delusional, Ripley.

But that surfer boy has put an impression on me. Something I know I can't shake off easily.

But, as Sandy has said, Cove is a bad boy. A player. A guy who doesn't care about who he hurts. A guy who is still hurting from his accident a year ago. A guy who doesn't want anyone close to his heart, not even his sister.

He's rude, arrogant, and cocky. A list of personality traits I most despised. I should hate him.

To put it bluntly, Cove is on the *very* bottom of the list of people I'd want to fuck right now.

When his bedroom door shuts close, Sandy turns to me.

"Now you see what we're dealing with here?"

"Oh," I reply with total conviction. "I definitely see."

6

RIPLEY

Waiting to meet Sandy and Cove's dad is much, *much* more stressful than I've anticipated.

"We'll sit at the back," Sandy tells the waiter at the restaurant, Rockpool, on the main street of New Water.

Sandy's taken me to her cousin's restaurant in order to meet her dad. The place is the biggest restaurant in town, serving seafood as its main specialty.

I follow the waiter as they take us to a booth in the back, Sandy's favorite spot.

"It's nice here," I say as I look around the beachy décor of the restaurant. It's late afternoon, only a few hours since I've landed from New York, and I'm still being amazed by everything in this country.

Sandy, seated, leans across the table towards me conspiratorially. "They have the *best* fish and chips here. You've got to try them."

I haven't realized how hungry I truly am. The last time I must've eaten was on the airplane, and that was crappy airline food. Some half-warm indigestible mac and cheese. I can't wait for a proper restaurant meal.

"Fish and chips is literally my favorite meal in the whole wide world," I reply to my best friend, taking a sip of the water the waiter has brought over.

Sandy chuckles to herself. "That's funny."

"What is?"

"Well, actually, you probably won't like this, but Cove's favorite meal is fish and chips as well."

I roll my eyes dramatically, causing Sandy to laugh again.

"Stop it, Ripley, stop making me laugh. You're gonna make water come out my nose."

She orders with the waiter for both of us. Two portions of Rockpool's finest fish and chips.

We spend the next ten minutes chatting about our lives. Sandy talks about her job at the elite private school and the troubles she has there. The other teachers look down at her because of her wealth; they just simply can't believe that she's made it as a teacher on her own merits, without her father's help or money. I reckon they're jealous of her and Sandy thinks they're just upset by the new blood coming in. They just don't like change, unable to deal with a new fresh face. Someone as young as Sandy working at the elite institution has somehow made them angry and resentful.

We also chat about my life and my dreams of becoming a nurse.

And we also talk about my life with Mom.

God, I'm already missing her so much. I wish she were here. I know Mom will absolutely love New Water. The quiet. The sunrise. The beautiful beaches. I know she would also love Sandy.

I really, really wished she were here to experience all this with me.

The food arrives on some very hot plates and it looks delicious. Fresh. Hot chips and battered fish done the Australian way.

"Straight from the ocean," Sandy says to me with a wink.

But no matter how delectable the fish and chips appear; I can't eat it. I can't stomach it at all. I'm just too nervous about meeting Sandy and Cove's dad. We're here at the restaurant to meet him, and yet my stomach is churning at the very thought of speaking to him. Mr. Finn is a renowned man for his short fuse and forthright manner, and I'm scared of being at the receiving end of his famous frankness.

Every time the restaurant door opens and someone steps in, I twist my head around to check if it's him. I'm on edge. Petrified. I need to calm down, but my jetlagged nerves aren't helping at all.

Sandy, sensing my rising discomfort, reaches across the table and takes my hand gently. "It's okay. It's just dad. I'm here too and I can deal with him for you. Don't worry about him."

She always knows the right thing to say.

Her and Cove's mom passed away a long time ago, just a year after Cove was born. We haven't really talked about it except for one time over Skype when Sandy opened up to me about it, and about how she practically had to step up to be Cove's mother because of it. I think it was pretty tough on her and Cove. Just goes to show that even the richest of families can have their own hardships.

The restaurant door opens, I turn my head, and in steps Mr. Finn himself.

He's here.

Michael Finn is the epitome of a suave billionaire businessman in his late sixties. Slicked-back white hair. A flashing smile. Tanned skin. Athletic body in a tight, expensive tailored suit. The man is a dictionary definition of a silver fox.

I can see where Sandy and Cove got their looks from. I can see where Sandy got her charm and where Cove got his arrogance. Michael Finn is both of those things. He strolls into the restaurant like he owns the place, shaking the hands of the waiters and chatting to some of the customers who recognize him. Well, technically, his family does own the place. His nephew, Cliff Finn - Sandy's cousin, is the owner.

Mr. Finn walks straight over to our table, widely smiling with his perfect white teeth at a passing waiter. As he passes, he orders the most expensive whiskey. One ice cube. Small glass.

"Ah, you must be Miss Ripley Sailor," the silver fox says, raising a manicured hand to shake mine. He's really turning on the charm taps here.

He's even more intimidating up close, just like Cove was this morning.

I nervously nod my head and shake his hand, feeling very aware of how sweaty my palm must be. Michael Finn has such a firm grip I'm worried he'll crush my hand. I can see how he's made so many high-flying deals; the man is born to be a billionaire businessman.

No wonder why Cove's so arrogant and sure of himself when he must've learned from the best.

"Hi, Mr. Finn. I'm Ripley."

"Oh, don't worry about my formal name. Only my employees call me Mr. Finn. Please call me Michael," he says, gesturing for me to sit back down. He turns to his daughter and gives her a kiss on the cheek. Michael Finn takes his seat. He seems to dominate the space. His booming voice and controlling manner made him the center of the room. Here is a man used to attention. The waiter arrives with his whiskey and Michael Finn thanks him with a ten-dollar tip.

"Thanks for coming, dad," Sandy says.

"Let's get straight down to business," Mr. Finn replies, taking a long sip of his drink. "Cove. He's why are here, he's why you've been taken from New York and flown down here, Ripley."

"Thank you for the trip, Mr. - Michael Finn," I say sheepishly. Sandy's dad waves my concerns away.

"No worries at all, Miss Sailor. Let me put everything to you bluntly. Cove's accident last year has cost me a lot of money. A *lot*. His recovery in the best private hospitals is one thing, but what's been going on recently is completely unacceptable."

"What dad's trying to say," Sandy explains to me, putting down a steaming chip. "Is that Cove is in a rough patch at the moment."

"A rough patch? More like a black hole," Michael Finn interrupts. "He *needs* to get back on his feet. Cove is an embarrassment, an utter embarrassment to me and the Finn family name."

"I wouldn't put it like that, dad."

"How else would you put it? He's gallivanting around town doing whatever drugs he can get his hands on and screwing any girl that gives him a second glance. He's completely out of control and it's ruining not just my reputation, but also yours, Sandy."

"I know, dad. But it's *not* embarrassment, it's more of a loss of his potential. He's a talented guy, he's just going... *nowhere*."

"Sure," Mr. Finn says, turning back to me. "Let's put it that way, then. Cove has a lot of potential. I see that in him. He wants to be a professional surfer rather than follow me into business, and it was really starting to come together until his accident at that surf competition when he threw his life away. He threw away everything. All his second chances. All the talent he has is going to waste, and now he's crashing at his sister's place. He has no job, no future, and I'm not prepared to keep on paying for his degenerate lifestyle."

"Dad, you're rambling on," Sandy says. She looks at me. "Basically, we want you to spend your time with Cove. That'll be his rent for living with me. We want you to do it."

I put down my knife and fork and glance at them both individually. "You know I'm not a psychologist, right? Let alone an actual nurse yet. Hell, I'm not even a proper nursing student yet. All I know is CPR."

Michael Finn leans forward so that he's inches away from my face. I can smell his expensive aftershave from here, probably something from one of the top places in Paris. "Cove has either screwed or given the silent treatment to every psychologist in the Southern Hemisphere," he whispers so that no one else in the restaurant can hear. "We need to do something unconventional, bring in *someone* unconventional. You're Sandy's best friend and she vouches for you. We need to do something different to get to Cove. And, plus, we need discretion when it comes to him and his... *activities*. I think you're perfectly suitable and fitting for the job."

"I know we can trust you, Ripley," Sandy says. "You're my best friend and you have such a good soul."

"We need discretion," Sandy's dad continues. "There's a lot of newspapers and tabloids out there that'll pay a lot of money to see a Finn fall flat on their drunken ass outside a nightclub. They'll pay a lot of money to find out Cove is in dire straits."

Sandy reaches across the table, squeezing my hand. She looks me directly in my eyes. I see unrestricted affection in hers. "We'll pay for your university fees," she says softly.

What? My university fees?

Does she know the magnitude of what she's saying?

It's unbelievable.

"What are you saying?" I ask, flabbergasted. "Everything?"

Sandy smiles. She knows what she's doing. "Yes, everything."

Images flash in my mind's eye. All my dreams achieved.

With my tuition fees paid for, I will have no more worries about where to get the money for my education, no more stress as I think about my future. My Mom can retire as soon as I get back home. She won't have to continue working night shifts as a nurse to get me through college. I'll be able to pay for it all. My life will be made infinitely easier.

Does Michael Finn and Sandy understand what they are offering means to me? What it will mean for my Mom? I very much doubt they do.

But it means everything.

I can't believe this.

But it'll mean staying here, in New Water, for six months. Six long months to get Cove back on his feet, back on a surfboard, and off his hedonistic lifestyle.

After seeing what he was like this morning, I have no doubts about the mountain I have to climb. This is going to be tough. Very tough. And it will probably, and in all likelihood it will be, *impossible*. I don't know if I will even succeed.

But the money for university is too big to ignore. Reforming Cove's life will give me security in mine.

I just have to do it, it's a golden opportunity I can't afford to waste.

Literally can't afford to waste.

Six months in New Water. Six months at Sandy's house.

Six months with Cove.

This is a big ask of me. From our initial meeting this morning, I know how hard it'll be to get to Cove in the way his dad wants me to.

How hard it'll be to change him.

I looked into Cove's eyes this morning and saw that the arrogant asshole doesn't want to change.

Sandy and her dad are putting all their trust in me, and I don't know how I can succeed.

Mr. Finn slicks back his gray hair with a hand. "Just keep Cove away from the drugs and that horrible nightclub. What is it called again, Sandy?"

"Tide."

"Yeah," Mr. Finn says. "Keep him away from Tide."

* * *

"PROMISE ME ONE THING," Sandy says to me as she drives her sports car with me in the front passenger seat back to her house from the restaurant. "One thing."

"What is it?" I ask.

"Just don't fuck Cove, okay?"

Huh?

I'm so taken aback in surprise I instinctively snort in derision, but from the stern look on her face, I realize that Sandy's being serious. "What do you even mean?"

"It's just that Cove seems to have this kind of *magical* effect on women. They all just fall head-over-heels at his feet."

Yeah, she's actually being serious.

"Sandy," I say, patting her on the shoulder. "Sandy, the

51

last thing I'm looking for is to get into bed with your younger brother. The last thing I'm looking for at the moment is sex, especially sex with Cove Finn. No offense."

"None taken."

"He's one hundred percent not my type. The very last thing I am planning for right now is falling head-over-heels over some rich stoner womanizing surfer boy, that's for sure," I reply. "No offense again."

"None taken."

We pull up at Sandy's house. The sun's setting low on the horizon. Streaks of red and orange light run across the sky in a beautiful pattern as the sun slowly bids farewell.

Yeah, Mom would love it here.

Before we even open the car doors, the front door of the house swings open, and out steps Cove.

My head whips around to face him.

Even I have to admit the man is *hot*. Gorgeous. Of course, he has women falling head-over-heels at his feet. He's naturally irresistible.

At least this time he's wearing clothes. It's not much, but at least it's some. A denim jacket and board shorts. At least it's better than what he greeted me in this morning.

I can still see his rock-solid abs under the jacket, his bare arms popping out, his bicep muscles hard in the sunset glow.

He casually strolls out of the house, flicking his hair back in a way that makes my sex shiver.

He's so *sure* of himself.

And yet so cocky. So arrogant.

I'm torn between despising his attitude and fawning over his perfect body.

Don't be such a little schoolgirl, Ripley. You know who he is. What he's like.

A narcissistic alpha dude chasing after the nearest available pussy.

Not my type at all.

He needs to learn some manners, especially after the dismissive way he treated me this morning at our first meeting. I want to teach him some respect.

"Where are you going?" Sandy asks him, getting out of her car.

Cove brushes past me towards a waiting taxi he's presumably just ordered. He doesn't even take a second look at me. He brushes past me like I'm nothing but a small fly in his way. "None of your business," he sneers at his sister.

"You're staying at my house rent-free, so it is my business," Sandy says. "Don't have a big night."

"Whatever, sis."

"You're going to Tide?"

Of course, the town's nightclub.

Of course Cove will be going there.

This must be some kind of routine for him. I bet he'll be waking up in bed tomorrow morning with a new girl he'll score in the club tonight.

But not on my watch, not after my conversation with his dad.

"Why do you care where I'm going, sis?" Cove asks Sandy, rolling his eyes.

Okay, I know this is my chance. I don't want Cove to think that I'm just some dumb American girl who has no backbone, some stupid Yank his sister brought over to stay like a charity school exchange program. I don't want him to think he can just brush past me like I don't matter.

This is my chance to stand up to the cowboy.

"Cove," I say forcefully enough to make him stop in his tracks. His hand on the taxi door halts. He turns back to me with a look in his blue eyes designed to kill, but I don't back down, not even under his intense glare. It's time for me to have a backbone. "It's time for us to get to know one another, so how about let's meet at the beach parking lot at six tomorrow morning? Bring your surfboard. Be there, Cove."

Cove doesn't reply. He turns away from me and ducks into the taxi, shutting the door after him.

But I know I've gotten to him, even if he doesn't want to show it.

I know he's thinking about me now.

I'm not just some stupid American crashing at his sister's place anymore, I'm more than that. I'm a threat.

I know Cove hasn't been on a surfboard in a whole year. He hasn't been on one since his accident, since that day at the Oceania Surf Competition.

I don't know anything about surfing, nothing at all, but I do know one thing.

I'm going to get him in the water and on a surfboard no matter what, if not for me, then for my Mom.

7

RIPLEY

"THAT'S SO good what you did out there," Sandy says, jumping in excitement as she closes the front door behind her. I can't help but match her bubbling energy.

"You think?"

"That's exactly what Cove needs, someone to kick him up the ass," Sandy exclaims loudly, throwing her car keys into a ceramic bowl sitting on the kitchen counter. They land with a satisfying *ding*. She's giddy, and I think it's because no one's stood up to her younger brother in the way I just did outside for quite some time. "Oh, I think I've made the right choice in bringing you here."

I smile, happy to see my best friend so happy. "I'm happy to be here."

"And I think you made the right impression on dad."

"Really?"

"I can tell he likes you, and he doesn't like many people."

"Oh, I'm honored."

I bow extravagantly, and Sandy laughs at my clownish display.

It's late, and I'm tired, but I'm happy I've restored my best friend's faith in me. The future's looking bright, and now all I have to do is deal with Cove in the morning.

The bad boy who wrecks hearts and bongs.

That will be the hard part.

I don't know what either Sandy or her dad see in me, but after my interactions with Cove, I don't think anyone can change him now.

"Let's have some wine," Sandy says, already heading over to the wine cabinet to pick out a bottle.

"Maybe not tonight, Sandy," I reply. "I'm still pretty tired from my trip."

She nods. "I understand. Go and get some sleep. You'll definitely need it dealing with my brother tomorrow morning."

I puff out my cheeks. "Tell me about it."

As I turn towards my room, something vibrates in my pocket.

My phone.

I take it out of my jeans.

MOM.

Her number flashes across the screen. She's calling me all the way from New York. I do the quick time zone calculation in my head and guess it must be super early back home, like sometime around five in the morning or something. This will be the first time we've been able to talk since I've landed, so I guess she wants to make sure I'm okay.

And I've missed her. I'm glad she's calling; I want to talk to her.

I need to hear the familiar sound of home after the day I've had today.

"It's Mom," I softly explain to Sandy. "I've got to take this."

She shoos me excitedly away into my guestroom, where I take the call.

"Mom," I say down the phone once I close my door. Her warm voice echoes through the phone and I immediately feel like I'm back in our little apartment together.

It's only been a few days, but I've really, really missed her.

Her questions come thick and fast, like the worried parent she is. "Ripley, how are you? Is the flight okay? How's Australia? How's Sandy? How is your first day?"

"Mom, slow down. Everything's fine. I'm great. Australia's great. Sandy's just great."

There's a lot of things I'm going to avoid talking to her about, even though it pains me. I don't want to talk to her about Cove, I don't want to have to explain him to her. I don't want to tell her that dealing with him seems impossible, and yet all the money for university depends on reforming him in just six months or fewer.

I don't want to tell her that I'm starting to think I've made the trip around the other side of the world for nothing.

Instead, I keep the phone call with Mom light and upbeat. I tell her about the wild dolphins I saw in the ocean, and I explain the beauty of Australia and this sleepy beachside town to her. I tell her about Sandy and what she's up to in her life and teaching career.

And I don't talk about Cove.

I just want to talk to her about good things. Nice things.

It's soothing to hear her voice. That heartening, familiar voice that makes the world seem a little bit safer. The voice of my mother takes me back to fond memories.

And, while I listen to her voice, I also remember the bad memories.

I remember that day when I was ten years old, that day I came home from school and saw my mother standing in our kitchen. Crying.

I'd never seen her cry before. She's usually so strong, so brave, but that day was different. *Something* was different. I knew instantly when I saw her that something had changed forever in our lives. Something bad.

I remember how, when she saw me, she turned to me in the kitchen and enveloped me in a big hug. She told me then that dad had left. He'd gone. My ten-year-old mind didn't comprehend it, couldn't understand what'd happened.

Dad's gone?

I asked Mom if dad was ever coming home. She told me no. She told me he found someone. Someone else. Someone different.

But me and her, she said that day, me and her are a team. We have each other, and that's what's important. We will stick together. We don't need him, or any man like him.

But I could still tell she was shattered. I could still tell that her spirit had been broken and that it would take years to heal.

I will never forgive my dad for what he did that day and for every day since. I never saw or heard from him again, and that's the reason why I will never trust someone - a man - like Cove Finn. That's why I will never trust a womanizing man because I know - I've had *experience* - that he will always leave the people he loves for that next hit. That next younger and prettier woman.

Cove Finn's behavior reminds me of my dad's that day when he left my Mom.

And I will never let a man do that to me. I will never let a man break me the way Dad broke Mom.

I will never allow that to happen to me.

After the phone call with Mom, I put the phone on charge and step into the en-suite shower. I find comfort in the hot water spraying down my back. I take the time in the shower to think about tomorrow, and what I need to do for the next six months.

It's going to be a lot of work with no guarantee of success, but I need to do it.

Cove Finn needs to change because I need the money. My Mom needs the money.

Mom and I – we've already dealt with one womanizing bastard before and I'm not going to lose to another. I'm not going to lose to Cove Finn.

8

COVE

WHAT IS this American girl on about?

Meeting up tomorrow morning at six?

Taking surfing lessons together?

Is she actually being serious?

What the actual fuck?

That *American* girl thinks she can humiliate me?

Who does she think she is?

I'm so pissed off by this strange little geeky girl and her early morning demands that by the time I drive over to Tide and stand outside its main doors, I decide to call my cousin. I know he'll be the only one who can understand me, the only one who'll understand the ridiculous situation I've been put in. He knows my family.

He's the only person who can talk to me with any respect.

"Cliff Finn you bastard!" I shout down the phone when he picks up. "What's going on?"

"Cove?" Cliff has a silky-smooth voice and I've always

reckoned he should work in radio. No wonder he charms all the babes around the world with his deep and lusty tones. "My playboy cousin, is that really you? You're calling me nice and early."

"Well, it's evening here," I reply, looking at the night-club. I've got a sudden urge for a drink, particularly a strong one. "Nice and early for you? So, where are you this time?"

I can practically *hear* Cliff smugly smiling down the line. "London, my friend. The city of royalty. I'm having an absolute blast of a time over here, Cove," my cousin barks at me and I chuckle along with him. Cliff always made me laugh, even in the worst of times. "What's going on at your end? You should come over here, mate. The champagne here is flowing and the girls go absolutely crazy for an Aussie accent. They all think we're Crocodile Dundee! I'm drowning in a sea of pussy here."

"Well, I'm actually in a bit of a sticky situation here myself, Cliff," I say. "And not the good pussy kind you seem to find yourself in."

Here goes.

Time to tell him. I close my eyes, cringing at the thought of today's events.

"Go on, Cove. What have you got yourself in this time?"

"Ah, it's my sister and Dad. They've gone mental this time, and I mean *proper* mental. Not just the usual crazy, but full-on psycho. They think I need help or something. Trust me, they've really got it in for me this time."

"Why? What's happened?"

"Right, so they've got this chick, some *American* chick - one of Sandy's friends or something - to fly over and stay with us, and I'm meant to spend time with her. They actually *want* me to spend time with her. Can you believe that?"

"Well, you know what I'll say to that, how there's only one important question. *Is she hot?*"

I shake my head in disgust, even though I know Cliff can't actually see me right now. "Let's just say she's not my usual type, that's for sure. She's essentially a geek, Cliff. She looks around the place so wide-eyed I'm worried she might trip over her own stupidity, and I don't think she's ever stepped a foot outside of Queens. She probably thinks she's in New Zealand or something."

My cousin laughs down the phone at my little joke. *Damn*, it's good to have an actual decent conversation with someone for once and not have them lecture you. All my dad and sister want to do is tell me how wrong I am in every facet of my life. At least with Cliff, I can just be my usual jokey self.

"Damn. Sucks for you, dude."

"Yeah, and the worst thing is that she wants me to take *surfing lessons*. The girl wants us to spend time together, like *actual* time. Like she's my therapist or something. Sandy told me she's here for six whole fucking months. Can you believe that?"

Cliff again laughs down the phone, and this time he's laughing at me. I cringe hard again. "Surfing? You haven't been surfing since the accident."

"I know."

"And she wants you to do it? That's pretty bold of her."

"That's what I think."

"So, what happens if you say no?"

"That's the fun part," I reply. "Apparently, according to my sister, my rent and trust fund are completely reliant on spending time with her and not fucking her about. They've really dug me into a corner here now, Cliff. It's like Dad and Sandy *want* me to hate them like they're actually pursuing my hatred. I'm thinking they get boners off my dislike of them."

"Yeah, that really sucks for you, dude," Cliff says. "What are you going to do about it?"

I rub my forehead. "I don't know yet. Probably pretend to play along and still go and do my own shit when she isn't looking. There's no way she can watch me twenty-four-fucking-seven. I need my booze, man, and my pussy."

"You know what I think?"

"What?"

"Well, it isn't my place to say anything."

I sigh. "You're my cousin, Cliff. You're, like, the only person on earth I can trust. Just tell me what you think."

"Well," Cliff paused. "I reckon it will be a good idea to just stick with the bitch and whatever she wants you to do for a few months just to get the money and recognition from your dad. Then, when this is all over, send her packing back to Queens or wherever she's from and go back to your normal life. Play the long game, Cove. Pretend you're their lap dog and do what this stupid American girl says and bide your time. You'll be back to fucking girls and getting high soon enough. Just ride out the storm, man."

I tut at how even Cliff is going along with Dad and Sandy's bullshit, but I hold my tongue. "Thanks for your advice, Cliff."

"No problem."

"Have a good time in London."

"Don't worry, I'll drink and fuck your portions as well as mine for the next six months. You go abstinent over there and I'll go crazy for you over here."

"Fuck off, you dick."

I hang up, despondent.

Yeah, finding out Cliff's on Dad's side is painful.

Ugh. Fuck me.

Can this day get any worse?

Meeting this American chick my sister brought over is

bad enough. I saw the look in her eyes when she met me, and the pity she looks at me with. Yeah, I was naked when I met her this morning, but so what? From the moment I saw her, I could tell she looks down at me. That's so rude. So disrespectful.

What a little geek. How dare some chick from Queens look down on me.

I saw straight through her the minute I noticed her standing in the middle of Sandy's kitchen. She's plain-looking. Brown eyes. Brown hair. Pale skin. So bland. Not even *fuckable*. I wouldn't even look twice at her in a nightclub.

And maybe that's why my sister brought her over; she knows there is no chance I will touch this geeky plain American girl even with a ten-foot-long jousting stick. My sister wants to tease me. Mock me.

Oh, and she's *succeeding*.

I immediately saw how my sister and my dad got to the American girl with their drivel. I bet dad lured her in with money. How sad.

She'll see soon enough that I'm a lost cause and that I don't deserve anyone's help, least of all hers. I've been nothing but a hopeless case since the accident and no one should feel the need to take care of me. Why can't they see I'm perfectly happy with what I'm doing now? I lost everything that day at the Oceania Surfing Competition. Everything.

Can't they just forget about reforming me and just let me live the way I want to?

If I want to end up each day drunk and stoned out of my mind with some random girl, then that's what I should be allowed to do; I don't want or need some American girl to be my cop.

Sandy thinks way too much of me and it's too much to

deal with. It's too much pressure to live up to. I'm not who I was a year ago. I'm not some world-class surfer on the cusp of glory, I'm just a world-class loser on the cusp of falling over drunk and high.

I don't deserve their help.

And, most of all, I don't want this stupid American girl in my life, especially not with that typical American sass she displayed as I left the house to come to Tide. She's the last thing I want or need.

She thinks she can boss me about. Well, no, sweetheart. Not me.

I look up at Tide. The familiar neon lights beckon me inside. I'm more at home amongst this crowd of party people than back in Sandy's home.

I don't need my dad. I don't need my sister. And I definitely don't need some Yank ruining the life I have going for myself.

I step up to the long line in front of Tide, the bouncer on the door waving me through the main door immediately, recognizing me.

"Thanks, Jim," I say, patting the nodding bouncer on the shoulder. The bouncers don't even take a second glance at me, or even care that I'm basically wearing nothing. I'm a fixture at Tide. Everyone who works here at the very least knows me, or even owes me something. Money, a favor. Something. With all the favors I've gathered here, I'm like a god in the nightclub, and it's my domain. I can do whatever, or *whoever*, I want within these four walls.

I'm king of the world, baby. *This world.*

The music of the club hits me before I even step inside. A loud throbbing beat, typical of this place. Once inside the darkness of Tide, I head straight for my usual spot, the VIP booth. It's my regular spot, always reserved for me. There's no one in this town more VIP than a Finn.

Everyone who spots me stops in their tracks and stares as I pass. They all know who I am, what my reputation is, my family's reputation. My family's money. I have a bad-boy reputation of being the richest guy in town and also the town's greatest failure. What a double whammy of accomplishments. Everyone knows what happened a year ago at the Oceania Surf Competition. Everyone knows who I am.

And I don't give a fuck.

There are a lot of rumors going around town about me. New Water's billionaire playboy failure.

And most of those rumors are true.

And I really, really don't care.

I pass by the dancefloor where people are rubbing up against each other, reveling in the music. Alcohol and drugs ran rampant here.

"Hey," someone grabs my wrist and holds on tight, whispering in my ear. Their breath is hot against my skin as I turn around to face them. It's a babe, a fucking *gorgeous* babe. She has great tits and a fuckable mouth and I'm instantly turned on. My cock twitches excitedly in my pants at the sight of her. She's very skimpily clad, just the way I like them. "Hey, are you who I think you are?" she asks, still whispering in my ear. My skin tingles with her being so close to me.

Oh, yes, she's *very* fuckable.

I smile at her. I know girls go wild for my smile. It's a weapon I deploy freely to much effect. "Depends on who you think I am."

"Let me guess," she bites her plump lips. Fuck, she's making *me* go wild. "Does your name start with C and end with E?"

I'm so fucking hard right now.

"You're right there, baby." I grab her around the waist and seductively pull her in towards me as she smiles at me, blushing. She wants me; I recognize that crazy feminine look of desire in her eyes anytime. I have her under my spell now. I feel her massive tits against my muscular chest.

This chick's definitely going to help me forget my problems, especially that American girl.

Screw Sandy and screw that American girl. Tonight's gonna be a good night.

9

RIPLEY

I'VE BEEN STANDING at the entrance to the beach parking lot for nearly an hour with no sign of Cove anywhere.

Nearly an hour. Waiting on my own.

A *whole* hour of standing by a bunch of cars watching surfers unpack their boards and apply sun lotion to their tanned Aussie faces, but not one sign of the one surfer boy I'm actually looking for.

A whole hour of waiting with growing impatience by the beach parking lot, but still Cove hasn't come.

I check the clock on my phone.

7 am.

Exactly one hour since we agreed to meet.

So. That's it.

He's a no show.

And that - *that* - makes me angry, so incredibly angry. The arrogance of the man to stand me up on our first morning together just makes my blood boil.

He thinks he can play me like that? He thinks he can play *games* with me?

Well, it takes two to tango, Cove Finn.

I can play games with him. I can strike back, and then he will see what this particular "American girl" is capable of and what I'm prepared to do.

At exactly one-minute past seven, I storm back towards Sandy's house, not stopping until I reach the front door. I pass by in the parking lot, without a second glance, the morning surfers and swimmers heading to the ocean. I know Sandy's already gone to her teaching job, so the house should be quiet. Cove should be in there, in his room, unless he's lying drunk in a ditch somewhere.

He'd better not be.

For his sake.

I unlock the front door and march straight on into the house, aiming directly at Cove's door.

I don't bother knocking.

I burst through into his bedroom with a slam of the door, not giving a damn about what he's doing in there. He could be smoking weed or sleeping or even masturbating, but I don't care right now.

Screw you, Cove, I'm coming in.

And, as I burst in, there he is, in his bed.

With a girl lying next to him.

A girl?

Her slender arms and toned legs are wrapped around the surfer whilst his body looks like he's trying to turn away from her. They are both fast asleep, but not for long. Not if I have any say in the matter.

This ends now, pretty boy.

"Cove!" I shout, waking them both up. "Cove!"

The handsome former surfer opens his eyes, moaning at the sudden intrusion into his bedroom and his sleep. *Good.*

He needs to pay, and I want to punch that stupid gorgeous face.

"What the fuck? What are you doing?" His voice is croaky and slurry from a night of drinking and sleeping and sex.

I put my hands on my hips. "Do you know what time it is?" I ask, voice dripping in such strong venom that it surprises me.

"I dunno," Cove replies with a loud yawn. "I guess the time's pretty fucking early, that's for sure."

"It's seven-thirty," I say, standing over his side of the bed. The girl next to Cove is rubbing her eyes. Both of them stink of sex. "You were meant to meet me at the beach parking lot at six, remember?"

"Oh yeah," Cove says with a smirk on his face. A *smirk*. The bastard. "That. Whatever."

"Whatever?"

"Yeah," Cove replies sleepily. His blonde hair is perfectly disheveled as he pouts his kissable lips. "Whatever. Just leave me be, girl, just let me sleep, Jesus."

Cove falls back to his pillow and shuts his eyes whilst I shake my head in anger. *God*, Cove is so much more a dickhead than I initially thought.

I look at the girl lying next to my best friend's handsome hunk of a brother. The girl is hot. *Real* hot. Big tits. Thick mouth. Of course, she's the type of girl Cove will sleep with. She's lying back in the bed taking absolutely zero notice of me. I'm nothing to her, just another plain girl annoying the man she's trying to ensnare.

But this particular plain American girl is not gonna stop at the first hurdle.

I look at them both nestled there in Cove's large bed, realizing now that this is the first time I've been in Cove's room, or even seen the inside of it. And the place is messy.

A filthy bombsite of a room. Dirty clothes hang everywhere. Nothing is in order. Cove evidently doesn't give a shit about the place he lives in. But this isn't just his place, this is *Sandy's* house, and he clearly has no respect for his sister's property. That pisses me off even more. After everything she's done for him, taking him in and paying for his lifestyle, this is how he repays her? Making his room an utter mess?

Wow, a real grade-one asshole.

My eyes land on the bedside table next to the girl. A large bag of green... something... lies next to a thick rolled joint. I know what it is.

Weed.

Jesus.

If all Cove thinks of me is that I'm some stupid loud American girl flying in to ruin his life, then I'm more than happy to play the part.

Time to wake up and face the music, surfer boy.

I lean in close to Cove's face. His eyes are still shut, but I know he's awake. I know he's just pretending in order to piss me off, and it's really working. I scan my eyes over his perfect cheekbones and his pronounced strong jawline. He's so goddamn *perfect*, a top-notch specimen of the male species, but he needs to be straightened out. He can't worm his way out of this with his beauty. *Oh no.*

Not with me, sunshine.

I take in a deep breath, preparing to use the full extent of my voice.

"There's going to be some ground rules that I'm going to set if you want me around," I shout loudly into his ear. Cove jerks back at the sound of my voice and blinks. He stares back at me with his cool blue eyes. "Number one, I am not going to do this if there's going to be a constant stream of girls entering and leaving your bedroom while I'm living under this roof."

Cove shakes his head in both disbelief and rejection. "What?"

I continue, ignoring his protests. "Number two, if you're going to be late again and make me wait in some parking lot for an *entire* hour for your sorry ass to show up, then there's going to be hell to pay."

"Wait, my sorry ass?"

"And number three." I point to the bag of weed and the joint on the bedside table. "If you smoke pot in front of me, then..."

"What?" Cove asks aggressively. "What are you going to do? Call my *daddy* on me?"

I stare back at Cove. "Precisely. That's exactly what I'm going to do. I'll call your *daddy* on you, and that'll mean that your money, your *inheritance*, will be gone. Forever. You can kiss all your money goodbye because with one call from me, then it's out the door, so I'll be pretty scared if I were you."

Cove waves his hands above his head in mock surrender. "*Ooooh*, I'm *so* scared. You terrify me *so* much, American girl."

"American *girl*?"

I've heard that insult from him too many times to simply ignore it now.

Cove rolls over away from me dismissively. "Come on, admit it, you need the money as much as I need it to continue living here rent-free, so how about you stop this American scout girl act and let's just stay out of each other's way? Collect your money and just let me be. Let me live."

Oh, I don't like his condescending tone one bit.

"Right," I say, leaning away from Cove's sculptured face and standing back up. "That's it."

I've had it with the rich surfer dude and his sarcastic ways with me.

I jump around to the front of Cove's bed and, in one move, grab the bedsheets and rip them off the two people lying there.

Take that, surfer boy.

"Hey!" the girl yells at me as Cove grunts in anger.

I don't care. I storm out of the room with his bedsheets under my arm. His room's a mess and I'm going to start to fix it, one bedsheet at a time. I don't even want to smell the sheets under my arm, so I don't dare inhale or breathe all the way out of the bedroom and into the living room.

I'm going to fix this.

No way do I agree with Cove and his silly plan. I'm not going to let him be and simply collect my money. I'm not going to lie to Sandy or to their dad and I'm not going to do this whole thing half-heartedly.

I'm all in, or I might as well head straight back home right now.

I take the bedsheets directly to the washing machine and I throw them in, starting the cycle without a pause.

Cove's following me. I hear him stomping right up behind me as I press the button to start the washing machine.

"And what the *hell* do you think you're doing?" Cove asks me from behind. I turn around to face him, relieving to see he's wearing some shorts for once. That's better than nothing. His tight abs are in my face and I can see the faint outline of his large cock under his shorts.

My pussy heats up at the mere sight of his massive cock's outline.

Stop. Don't think about him like that, Ripley. Don't you dare think about him naked.

"Look, we both need the money," I explain to him. "And, as much as I hate to admit it, we need each other. We can get through this as long as we communicate, and as long

73

as you don't keep me waiting in some parking lot for an hour. If we do the right things and we both please your dad and sister, then we both benefit, so let's work together, okay? Does that sound good? Can we work together and get this done?"

The little spiel hasn't come out as well as it was formulated in my head, but Cove gets the main gist of it.

Cove pauses as he takes it in. I can see his anger subsiding. He's thinking about it, about what I've said.

He takes one last look at me, one last look with those blue eyes of his that remind me of the wild blue ocean. Those same eyes I can just melt in.

And then he grunts, turning around and walking out of the room. I hear the slamming of his bedroom door a moment later.

Great. Just great.

I think I've got through to him. I think I've made my point, but not as clear enough as I wanted it to be. So, Cove is determined to fight me on this to the bitter end?

I can't fight this. I'm not up to this.

I'm resigned now. Judging by his reaction, this is going to be impossible.

Completely impossible.

Six more months. Six more months of *this*?

No way.

I can't do it.

10

RIPLEY

THAT'S IT, no more Cove and no more Australia.

I've given up.

I'm going home.

I wait for Sandy to return from school. Cove - and that random party girl he'd brought home last night - has disappeared. Gone since this morning. I don't know where they went and, to be honest, I don't care anymore. I haven't seen surfer boy since he grunted incoherently at me and ran away from me when I tore off his bedsheets. I didn't go searching for him; he's a big boy and he can handle himself, and besides, I decided that this wasn't my fight anymore.

Cove is no longer my fight.

He can do whatever he wants now. I'm going home.

In the hours since Cove disappeared, I've just been sitting around Sandy's home. I made myself a sandwich and opened up one of the nursing textbooks I've lugged all the way to Australia in case I got free time to study. I've had a lot of time to think today whilst Sandy has been still at work. Time to think about my future in this country.

And now my mind is made up.

There isn't a future for me here in Australia.

If you look up the word *impossible* in the dictionary, I bet you a hundred bucks Cove's face will be printed in the definition. I can't deal with him anymore. It hasn't even been a full day and I'm already over him. No way can I stand six more months of this.

I'm going home.

Back to Mom and back to more debt and financial stress, but that doesn't matter. I can't do what Sandy and her dad are asking me to do. It's impossible, I can't fix Cove Finn.

And that's what's led to me sitting at the kitchen counter with my nursing textbook opened to the section about CPR when I hear the familiar sound of Sandy's car pulling up in her driveway. I hear the car door closing, and then the scratching sound of Sandy unlocking her front door.

She has no idea what she's stepping into here.

This morning, after Cove left, I decided not to message my best friend about my decision to go home. Instead, I wanted to talk to her in person. She deserves that respect. Even if her brother doesn't.

"Ripley!" Sandy shouts my name as she walks in, throwing her keys in the ceramic bowl. She's happy to see me, but I doubt my face reciprocated her joy. She notices that pretty quickly and her voice immediately goes quiet, knowing something's happened with her best friend. "What's wrong? How was your first day with Cove?"

I sigh and shrug my shoulders. "Do you have any wine?" I ask.

Sandy's face and mood changes, her smile turns upside down. "That bad, huh?"

I nod. "Yeah."

"Well," Sandy replies with a smile. "Good luck for you that my favorite drink is Chardonnay and that I have plenty of that stocked up in my house." She skips over to the fridge and pulls out a bottle of white wine, brandishing it like a trophy she's won. I can tell she's refusing to let my sour mood ruin the evening, even if I have bad news. "Let's open this baby."

She eagerly pours the wine into two very large glasses she finds in the cabinet. I close my nursing textbook and we sit down at the dinner table to talk with the wine glasses Sandy has practically filled to the brim, ready to drink in front of us.

"Tell me everything," she says, reaching out to take my hand sympathetically.

I sigh. Again. I don't want to give my best friend bad news, especially not when she's looking at me with such a caring and hopeful look. She's done so much to get me to Australia, and I don't want to let her down, but I have to. My mind's made up. "I'm thinking of going home, Sandy," I say. "This is too much for me. Cove is impossible, this is impossible. What you're asking me to do these next six months is impossible."

Sandy blinked. "What are you saying?"

Time to spill it.

"I'm saying I'm going home," I reply. I feel her hand rub on mine and it makes me sad. I don't want to be saying this, but it's the truth, and that's what Sandy deserves from me. "I admit defeat. I quit. I failed. I'm so, so sorry, Sandy, but I've had enough. I promise I'll pay for my few days stay here and then I'll get the first flight out in the morning. I'm just so, so sorry for all the trouble I've caused."

Sandy doesn't speak for a long time. She picks up her glass of wine and gulps it down in one go, drinking it like it is water. I'm amazed at her drinking ability. Done, she slams the empty glass on the table with a bang. "No way," she says defiantly. Her tone is unwavering and strong. "No fucking way, Ripley. You're not giving up, not yet. Not if I have anything to say about it. You, Ripley Sailor, will wait here. I'm sorting this whole situation out. Cove can't get away with this."

Then, without waiting for me to protest or even ask what she's doing, Sandy gets up from her seat and, in a quick flurry of movement, snatches her car keys from the ceramic bowl. She flies out the front door and launches the car out of the driveway and onto the road with a spin of her tires.

She's gone, leaving me sitting in her living room with my half-drunk glass and Sandy's empty glass of Chardonnay in front of me.

She wants me to wait here? She's sorting this whole situation out?

What the hell's Sandy doing?

11

COVE

Screw my Dad.

Screw Sandy.

And, most of all, screw Ripley Sailor. The girl who's given me hell.

The American girl has caused me too much trouble than she's worth. Take this morning; it was an absolute *disgrace*, coming into my room like that. Like, who does she think she is?

Some geeky American girl who thinks she can control me?

Although I have to admit I felt pretty goddamn attracted to her when she pulled her little stunt this morning, it's strange, but true. When she confidently and sassily pulled off my bedsheets and stormed off in her adorable pouty way, I did feel a ping of desire deep in my body.

Damn it. She's getting to me.

I liked the way she did that, and she did look hella cute with my bedsheets trailing after her perky little *holier-than-*

thou ass. Her body isn't bad. In fact, it's pretty hot if she didn't hide it behind those layers of cheap clothes she likes to wear.

No girl has ever stood up to me like the way Ripley has. Usually, girls just fawn over my Adonis-like body and throw themselves at my feet. Most girls prefer to suck my massive cock than even dare to tell me no. No girl until this Ripley Sailor has fought back at me whilst not giving a damn what I think. Tearing my bedsheets off like that instantly makes her ten times bolder and assertive than most girls I've ever come across, and, *damn*, I like assertive girls.

Ah, stop it, Cove.

I've gotta remember she's nothing but a spy my family has hired to keep a close eye on me, and the absolute last thing I need to be doing is actually *falling* for the enemy. The goddamn last thing I need to do is to actually fall for *Ripley fucking Sailor.*

But my heart's pretty torn over this strange girl who's just come into my life. But I can't let my emotions, or my dick, force me into actually *caring* for the girl.

And that's why I've ended up this evening back at Tide. The nightclub is my safe haven, my harbor. In the safety of the neon lights and overpriced alcohol, I find my solitude away from my restrictive family and their cute American spies. Tide is my real home.

I sit in my usual spot, the VIP booth. I'm roped off from the rest of the nightclub but I'm not alone; surrounding me are half a dozen girls circling like vultures for my attention and by my side is my weed dealer offering me puffs from a thick joint he's just rolled.

This is my usual position, and this is where I felt right at home, not in my sister's house with that American girl tormenting me, no matter how cute or attractive I found her.

She'll have your balls, Cove if you're not careful. Don't fancy the enemy.

"Dude, try this one," says my weed dealer - some guy named Kev - as he reaches across the booth and offers me a new joint. I reach over the massive tits, barely hemmed in by her dress, of the gushing girl sitting next to me and take the offered joint between my fingers. The girl's hands are all over me, but I ignore her. She isn't interesting to me at all, which is *very* unusual, especially with her inflated body. The kind of body I usually go for. Instead, my mind is stuck on that Ripley Sailor and the pretty way she smiled at me when she cockily ripped those bedsheets off my bed this morning.

No way do I actually like this intruding American girl. She's not my type at all.

I'm very confused, and Kev's powerful new joint isn't going to help.

"Excuse me," I call out to a passing waitress, one I've met in the club a few times before. I can't remember if I've slept with her or not yet. She turns and smiled in my direction. Okay, I clearly *haven't* slept with her. If I had, I wouldn't have gotten a smile from her. Instead, I would've most likely have gotten a slap to the face. "Your best bottle of vodka and enough shot glasses for the table as soon as possible."

"Certainly, sir," the waitress purrs at me, and I quickly made a mental note to talk to her in the next few days. She's now high on my target list. I bet she'll be in my bed before the week is out.

See, Cove? You can forget about the American girl if you just try hard enough.

I don't need to think about Ripley *fucking* Sailor when I have plenty of girls racing to be under my bedsheets.

"Tell us a surfing story," the girl with the massive tits

next to me asks, one of her hands busily rubbing my solid abs. I laugh and don't say anything. Her friend next to her reaches over and joins her friend in playing with my exposed muscular torso.

Yeah, I definitely don't need no Ripley Sailor in my life when I have all the pussy I want.

Screw Dad. Screw Sandy. And screw Ripley Sailor.

It only takes a moment for the waitress to return with a giant vodka bottle, carrying it in on a tray surrounded by lit sparklers. It's a big display that causes the rest of the club to turn their necks and stare. The vodka and sparklers are the centerpieces, but really, *I'm* the attraction to these clubgoers. The Finn who fucked up his surfing career and is now the town's rich loser asshole.

That's me.

The waitress whoops and excitedly brings the vodka over to me to drink.

Stop thinking about Ripley Sailor, just forget about her.

I gesture for the waitress to pour the bottle directly into my mouth. She does so, giggling. I open my lips and let the clear, strong liquid in. Yeah, I'm an expert in drinking. The waitress whoops again and jiggles her tits in my direction.

She pulls the bottle back away from my mouth and I swallow the alcohol, winking at her. She winks back.

Then I turn to the rest of the booth.

And what I see nearly makes me spit out the vodka still stored in my mouth.

My sister, *Sandy Finn*, is standing in the booth. Standing there amongst the girls and my weed dealer, staring at me with her hands on her hips.

Shit.

To my knowledge, Sandy has never stepped a foot inside Tide. This place isn't her scene at all, and I've never even seen her near the front doors. She hates this place, and the people associated with it in the town. This club is off-limits to her.

And yet she's still here, standing in the middle of my VIP booth and staring at me with a look that can launch a thousand daggers into my heart.

Shit.

"Sandy?" It's all I can say.

She turns away from me to take in all the girls, my weed dealer, and the waitress I've been flirting with. "Everyone out, now," my sister says in a tone I've rarely seen her use. No one in the booth moves, mostly out of shock and the fear of another member of the Finn family standing so imposingly over them. "Do you lot want my dad to get involved?"

That's more than enough to send them packing. In seconds, everyone has hastily scrambled out of the VIP booth, including the waitress, leaving just me and my sister alone.

"I didn't think so," Sandy says to herself triumphantly.

Aw, she's made everyone leave.

"What do you want, sis? Why have you come here?" I ask my sister dismissively. My initial shock is over and now I'm starting to get pissed off. Sandy has sent my friends and my potential fucks away, ruining my night before it's even properly begun.

"You're coming home. Now."

I shake my head. "No."

"What?"

I sit back down and lean against the soft leather back of the booth, exaggeratingly putting my foot up on the table and knocking off a shot glass. Sandy watches on with contempt. "I said no, I'm not coming home. Not now."

I know what she's talking about and why she wants me home.

It's all to do with Ripley Sailor.

That pretty girl's gonna be the death of me.

Sandy sits down next to me in the booth, looking me deep in my eyes. "You know that Ripley is your last chance, right? Your *very* last chance. If you don't do what Dad wants you to do and spend time with her and follow-through, then he will disown you. He will make you home-less, and that's it. She's your last chance, and she's already thinking of flying back to America in the morning. If she gets on that flight, then all your money goes out the door with her. Gone forever, you get me?"

I sigh. "Right."

"So please," Sandy says, leaning towards me. She's being sincere. She's actually pleading with me. "Please come home."

I think about the nightclub. I think about the waitress and how we'd winked at each other.

I think about Ripley cutely pulling off my bedsheets this morning.

"Fuck it," I reply, resigned.

Ripley Sailor wins this round.

* * *

We don't listen to music on the drive back home. I sit in the passenger seat next to Sandy in her expensive sports car as we wind through the hilly streets and beachside roads of New Water to get back to her place. We don't even speak a word with each other the whole journey.

I'm only doing this because she pleaded with me so earnestly in the club.

I'm only doing this because I need the money that my dad threatens to withhold.

I'm definitely *not* doing this for Ripley Sailor, no matter how cute I found her little act of defiance this morning.

Definitely not for her.

We arrive back home with a hard brake that makes me slam into my seat. I think it's on purpose; my sister can drive real fast when she wants to. Sandy unlocks the door and we both walk into her house.

Here we go.

That American girl is sitting at the table, a half-drunk glass of white wine in front of her. She watches me enter with a cold look on her face.

Fuck it. Let's get this over with.

I stroll right up to her. "Fine then," I say as I pick up her glass and drink the rest of the wine contained within it in one go. Drinking the rest of her wine is my one little act of defiance. The drink's warm; she's been sitting here for some time, then. "Have it your way."

The American girl looks up at me with those big brown eyes of hers.

"You're seriously doing this?" she asks, not remarking on the fact I've just drunk her entire wine glass.

"There's no way in hell I'm going surfing," I reply. "But I can agree to teach you instead. Is that good enough for you?"

She flashes me her teeth in a wonky geeky smile that is kinda adorable. "It's perfect," she says.

She really isn't my type, but she's actually super appealing to me.

"I'll see you at ten tomorrow morning, then. Sandy will give you one of her wetsuits to wear."

"No, the lesson will be at six in the morning."

What? Defying me again?

The balls on this girl.

Damn, this girl doesn't know when to stop, does she? She actually likes saying no to me.

No one says no to me.

"Okay, I'll see you at nine, then."

"Let's make it seven," she replies. She's harder than she looks. "And that's final."

Fuck me, she really does have balls.

I have no option but to snarl at her like a wolf and storm off into my room.

Before I shut the door, I overhear Sandy saying to Ripley, "I think that's a yes, then."

Screw those girls.

12

COVE

THE WIND WHIPS through my wavy hair as I look out across the beach and at the early morning sun. The concrete steps leading down from the parking lot and into the sand are cold and rough on my feet. The white sand below beckons me; it wants me to step down on it, feel it.

But I'm frozen to the spot with trepidation.

The beach. I'm here.

I'm back.

It has been a long time since I've last set foot on sand, a whole year since that accident at Oceania Surf Competition. I haven't felt the sand since; I haven't been on a beach since. I've missed it.

But I don't deserve to be here.

I flick my blonde hair back and squint towards the ocean. The sun's rising and I can just make out the early morning surfers bobbing up and down on the waves in the distance.

I wish I were out there again, tasting the salt in my

mouth, feeling the cold water splash against my wetsuit, feel the touch of a surfboard again.

That would be perfect.

But I don't deserve to.

I failed a year ago.

I fucked up.

I don't deserve the feel of the ocean.

I'm not meant to be back on a beach during sunrise with a board under my arm. I'm supposed to be back in bed.

I'm at the beach before that American girl's even here. She'll be surprised by that. She thinks that I'm just some lazy stoner dude, but I'm used to waking up early to catch the first wave from when I'm a kid. An early morning trip to the beach is as natural to me as breathing. It's just that I haven't done it in a year.

A whole year of avoiding this place. Avoiding who I am.

Everything in my life came crashing down because of my screw up at that surf competition a year ago. The super-model girlfriend I had left me by a text unceremoniously, my dad hates me, and my sister thinks I'm a joke.

I flick back my hair again.

It is good to be back on the beach, though.

I look back down at the beach and reach out with my foot. It makes contact with the warm sand.

Home.

A shiver goes up my body as memories flood back. All those childhood lessons. All the times I will full-on dash into the cold ocean water with my surfboard in my hands, eager to feel the waves on my body and taste the saltwater in my young mouth. The smell of hot sun cream. Everything about the beach reminds me of good times and makes me happy.

And then I remember the accident; the falling from the surfboard in front of everyone, the massive wave that crashed into me like a wall of bricks, being unconscious and having to be pulled out of the water by the lifeguards. Sitting in that hospital bed for weeks as I recovered from surgery. The two long scars on my legs. The look on my dad and sister's faces as they sadly stood around my hospital bed staring at my broken body. And, most of all, that feeling of failure, that feeling that I fucked up everything that fateful day and how I can never go back to the way things were.

Both of my feet are on the sand.

Here I am.

I'm standing on the beach for the first time in a year.

And it feels good.

I turn back around to look at the car park behind me. I can make out someone coming towards me, strolling down the hill towards the steps onto the beach.

It's *her*. The same girl who thinks she can change me, shape me back to who I was. The girl with sass, who thinks she can defy me. The girl who's actually kinda cute.

That cocky little preppy American girl.

She's here.

Ripley fucking Sailor.

13

RIPLEY

I DON'T EXPECT Cove to be there at the beach before I am. That's pretty surprising.

But it's good to see him standing on the beach, looking every part the surfer boy I know he is.

I bite my lip when I spot him. He's wearing nothing but his tight board shorts that are just *begging* to be ripped off.

Hot damn.

He looks so strong standing there with his muscular arms crossed and with the rising morning sun behind him, his medium-length bleach-blonde hair swaying softly in the ocean breeze. The way his blue eyes spot me from across the parking lot makes my stomach turn into such tight knots that I just know will be nearly impossible to untangle.

God, he's so handsome.

Typical me to start fancying the hot asshole.

He's that cocky surfer dude I endlessly dreamed and fantasized about when I was a little girl. The guy who's so confident and sure of himself and his abilities, especially in the ocean. The guy who can easily pick you up in his strong arms and sprint into the sea without any strain. The guy who doesn't give a shit about anyone else except for you. Only you.

The cocky and confident guy I used to dream about is standing right *there* at the bottom of the steps leading onto the beach.

Cove Finn is one hell of a hunk, and the sight of him makes my little heart flutter like a butterfly.

No, Ripley. You know what he's like.

A heartbreaker.

A player.

An asshole.

A guy who doesn't care about anything other than where the next hit of pleasure is coming from, whether that's from a joint or from a girl.

Remember who he is.

Cove Finn is *dangerous*. Dangerous for the job I'm hired by Sandy to do, but most of all, dangerous for my heart.

And now I'm walking straight towards him. Towards danger.

Towards Cove Finn.

"Hello, American girl," he greets me as I skip down the stairs and feel my feet reach the warm sand of the beach. I refuse to be dragged into his little games, so I ignore his snarky nickname for me. Today is more important than to be annoyed by Cove Finn's taunts.

"You ready, then?" I ask.

Cove raises a curious eyebrow. "Ready for your first surfing lesson?"

"Yeah."

"Only if you are." Cove brushes past me back up the stairs, beckoning me to follow with a wave of his hand. I roll my eyes and chase after him as he strolls quickly across the parking lot and towards his car. He pulls off a small surfboard that's securely fastened to the top of the car and throws it towards me. I catch it awkwardly. The thing is lighter and smoother than I anticipated.

"Is this your surfboard?" I ask, feeling the edge of the thing.

Cove points at it. "This is the first surfboard I ever owned, back when I was a teenager."

His first-ever surfboard? I like that. It makes me feel like I'm holding onto a bit of his soul in my hands. I like how he shares that fact with me. This thing must be super precious to Cove and yet he's allowing me to use it. I kinda felt honored.

The surfboard's a piece of his history.

"So, you had this as a teenager? I find it hard to imagine you as a teenage boy."

"Why?" Cove asks, stepping towards me. "Do you think if we met as teenagers, you'd fancy me?"

I snort. "As if you would be so lucky, Cove Finn."

"I'm sure I could've worked my magic on your geeky ass."

Yeah, to be honest, I bet he would've. And it probably would've worked.

"In your dreams, pal," I reply. "So, what were you like as a teenager?"

"Why do you want to know?"

"We're going to be spending the next few months together," I say, shrugging. "We might as well get to understand each other."

Cove turns and stares out at the ocean. "It was mostly surfing. That's all I did as a teenager," he replies. "Other than that, I was a pretty shy kid. I never really liked talking."

I punch his arm playfully; I can't imagine him being a

shy kid at all. Not that cocky Cove I know. "Shut up, I bet you weren't. I bet all the girls wanted to date Mr. Surfer Boy."

He laughs and turns back to face me with his piercing blue eyes. "No really, it's true. It's pretty strange being the rich kid in a small town. I just stuck to surfing all the time. Surfing gave me a way out of just being the kid with the rich dad and it instead gave me something to excel in. It's something different from my dad and my family's expectations. See, you don't really know me at all."

Oh, there's more to him than I initially thought. He's not just an arrogant dick.

"Maybe you can still do it."

Cove winces. "Surfing?"

"Yeah," I reply. "You can try it again, see if you've still got it."

His face changes. He's no longer laughing. "No, Ripley." His voice is direct and unmoving, it's clear he doesn't want to talk about him getting back on a board anytime soon.

I've pushed him too far.

I get it now. He's still hurt from his accident. His body might've recovered, but he's still healing inside. Getting him to even teach me surfing is already a big step for him. I can't also get him to open up already to all his past wounds.

The message from him is loud and clear.

Don't try to get him back on a board.

Cove still needs more time.

"Okay."

"How about we head down to the beach, then?" Cove suggests, breaking the tension.

With his teenage surfboard under his arm, Cove leads me back to the steps leading down into the sand. I can taste the salt from the ocean breeze already. With the heat and the clear blue water and the sheer openness of it all, this is a foreign land for me, but, looking up at how self-assured Cove is as he walks towards the beach, I can tell it's natural for him. This is a guy in his element. I just wish I could see him actually surf, see him doing the thing he was actually born to do.

I bet he's an amazing surfer.

Sandy told me how he used to be the best. The way he danced on the waves was apparently the best she's ever witnessed. I really wish I could see that for myself.

As we reach the area where the parking lot ended and the grass before the beach started, someone steps into our path.

"Cove?" It's a man coming back from the beach. He's wearing a black wetsuit, dripping wet from the ocean. His dark hair sticks to his forehead. He's around the same age as Cove and me, early twenties. He carries a long surfboard under his arm. "Cove Finn?"

I glance at Cove next to me as the man rushes up to us, his surfboard flapping in the breeze. He's one of the early morning surfers, and both Cove and I are forced to stop as he approaches, blocking our path to the beach. I watch as Cove narrows his eyes at the stranger.

"James?" Cove asks the surfer, slowly recognizing the man.

"Long time no see, Cove," James the surfer says, coming to a stop in front of us. He's a big guy, nearly as tall and muscular as Cove. *Nearly*, but not quite. "How long has it been, mate?"

"Nearly two years," Cove replies, still hesitant.

I don't think he likes this.

"Yeah, nearly two years."

"I heard about your accident, and about everything since. What a fuck up, hey."

I sense Cove stiffening next to me. This James guy is pretty forward. He seems like a dick to me, and I think that Cove thinks the same. "Yeah."

James wipes some ocean water from his forehead. "I remember how you are always out there in the ocean even earlier than the old pros, but that was back when you are a teenager. Now, look at you. Now I've heard about how you're scared about going into the water. Everyone says you're a chicken, and that the waves freak you out or something. Is that really true?"

Cove doesn't reply. I look up at him and at his perfect face. He's tensing up. His muscles are rock solid as he grows angry. I don't like it.

This James guy is a total *dick*.

James laughs, sensing how much he's embarrassing Cove. He's enjoying this. "You fall off once, and now the famous Cove Finn is scared of the water? How time's change, hey?"

James' eyes catch sight of the scars on Cove's legs. Smiling, he shakes his head.

He's laughing at Cove. Laughing at his accident.

And Cove is frozen to the spot.

James, sensing weakness, continues on the mocking attack.

"And who's this then?" he asks, turning to me. I shirk back from the man, taking a step back. He's intimidating as hell and an aggressive man to boot.

He scares me.

Screw him, and screw how he's treating Cove. He can fuck about with Cove Finn, but he isn't going to intimidate or insult me.

I'm not going to back down.

"I'm Ripley Sailor," I say, offering out my hand.

In a snort of derision, James doesn't take it.

It's like I'm worth nothing.

He ignores me.

He turns back to Cove.

"Well, Cove," he says in a condescending tone. "I also heard you are fucking all the girls in town, but I don't expect you to be going after even the ugly American sluts."

THRACK!

The punch happens so fast I don't have time to register it before it's over.

Cove has punched James.

He's punched him in the face.

The guy in the wetsuit stumbles back, covering his nose with his wet hand. He squeals in shock.

Cove's hand is still outstretched, his fingers closed in a fist. It's a perfect punch thrown by a strong man. Swift and direct. Full of anger and energy.

James never stood a chance.

Cove's punched James? Because he insulted me?

I'm in shock.

That's until Cove turns to me and takes my hand in his, pulling me away from the scene, pulling me back towards the car.

Cove's big hand is warm against mine. He's so *big*, so *strong*. And I realize then that this is the first time Cove has touched me. He hadn't shaken my hand when we were introduced, but now my hand is within his. My stomach flutters.

Holding tightly onto my hand, Cove pulls me back to his car. We jump into the vehicle in a rush. My heart's beating heavily. Once in the car, Cove immediately hits the pedal and we zoom screeching out of the parking lot, Cove traveling at such fast speeds I'm worried we'll be pulled over by a cop.

I don't realize I'm breathing shallowly until I'm safely

reclining in the leather car seat racing away from the beach. I face Cove sitting in the driver's seat next to me.

The man is a perfect picture of calm restraint, his hands smoothly operating the steering wheel and the stick, his eyes scanning the road. He doesn't seem perturbed by what has just occurred. He doesn't seem fazed that he'd just actually *punched* someone in the face.

"What happened?" I ask him through my shallow breaths. "Why did you do that for?"

Cove doesn't take his eyes from the road. "I didn't like what he said about you," he replies softly, under his breath. "I *hated* what he said about you. You're not a slut and you're not ugly, so he had to pay for what he said about you."

He punched James for me?

Cove doesn't look concerned. He turns the car onto another winding road, heading up over a hill. His driving is immaculate, even though he's going at super-fast speeds.

He was defending me?

"Aren't you worried about him?" I ask, trying to slow down my hasty breathing. I close my eyes and focus on my heartbeat. Everything's happened so quickly and I'm still processing it. "Aren't you worried about repercussions, or about the police? Or what people will think of you?"

Cove laughs. A deep laugh, as if I've said something stupid. "Ripley," he says. "I'm the bad boy of New Water. My image is already tarnished, and my reputation is already ruined. There are no repercussions to worry about. James will be terrified of me. Plus, if he does pursue me, he'll have to deal with my family if he gets the police involved." Cove turns to me and smiles.

The cocky bastard.

The *handsome* cocky bastard who's punched a guy just because he insulted me. My common sense is telling me it's stupid to find that behavior chivalrous, but my heart is finding it *very* sexy. Cove's risking arrest to defend my honor.

It's kinda hot.

Plus, Cove has said I'm not ugly. That's the best thing he's said to me so far. It's a *big* improvement over what he's said over the last few days. I mean, it isn't exactly Shakespeare or anything, but it still makes my heart skip a few beats.

No. Cove is still Cove. Yeah, he might've punched a guy for calling me a slut, but he's still the rebel bad boy. He's still a heartbreaker. He doesn't care about me, he doesn't care about anyone but himself.

"Where are you taking me?" I ask.

He turns the car right onto another road. We zoom along the asphalt. There are no other cars on this road, and I realize we are heading further out of town, further up the coast. "We're going to a secret beach that no one else knows about except for me," Cove replies.

"A secret beach?"

"Yeah, no one knows about it, not even Sandy. I used to go here as a teenager. It's a bit out of the way but I'll find it. I just want to get away from the crowded beach."

"You're taking me to a secret beach?"

This is crazy.

"Yeah. But don't worry, this place will be better for your surfing lessons, anyway."

"Oh, great."

I'm going to an empty beach with Cove. Him and me. Alone.

Cove turns back to me and looks at me deeply with his bright blue eyes. "No one will find us here."

We will be completely alone.

14

RIPLEY

"Trust me."

I glance from Cove's outstretched hand and up to his blue eyes, staring back at me like pools of clear tropical water.

Yeah, I trust him.

Especially after what he did with that James guy.

"I've done this path a thousand times before," Cove continues, his voice soft and tender. He's talking to me, directly to me, like we're close friends. "Trust me."

I realize right now that I do trust Cove. Totally.

Oh God, what have I turned into? Another one of his fawning female conquests?

"Okay," I reply, taking his hand. I feel his soft, tanned skin on mine. He grips my hand tightly, just like he had back at the beach parking lot, and it makes me feel so safe.

I do trust him.

I'm beginning to wonder if Cove actually likes me. Like, does he *like* me? After all, he did punch a guy in public for insulting me, so you can't blame me if now I'm beginning to suspect there's more to Cove than the outer rebel playboy exterior he likes to show off. He's been different to me all morning.

Maybe he actually cares about me?

I mean, he's actually taking me to a place he's never taken anyone else before, especially not other girls. So, what makes me different from the legion of temporary girl-friends he'd had before? And does Cove even view me as special?

Maybe I am.

Maybe he's thinking of me as more than just some annoying American girl he has to keep around to keep getting his rent money.

Why else would he be acting so protective and caring? Showing me places he's never shown anyone else?

I certainly feel special.

But maybe that's his way with every girl, maybe that's his trick. Make them feel special.

Sandy did say he has a tricky way with women, that they fall at his feet.

Oh, god, is that what I'm doing now?

Does it just take Cove reaching out and taking my hand at the end of some Australian bushland to melt my weak heart? Is that all it takes?

Well, it's certainly working.

Oh, God.

"Follow me," he says, smiling that gorgeous smile that can somehow make my entire body shudder. He pulls me away from his parked car and into the thick bushland. We've arrived at this spot along a bit of dirt road only minutes before. I thought Cove was lost, but he told me we were at the entrance to his secret beach. I didn't believe we were actually at a beach; I still don't believe him because all

I can see is nothing around us but thick foliage leading to more foliage. No beach in sight.

But Cove is so confident and persistent and dreamy looking that I just have to follow him.

And so I do, with his hand around mine, into the Australian bush heading into god-knows-where.

You're going into a forest with a strange man, Ripley Sailor. How dumb are you?

No wonder no one else knows where this secret beach is. You have to be Tarzan to find it.

But guide me through the dense foliage Cove does, over slippery rocks and twisted branches all the way downhill. I don't know where we are going, but Cove certainly seems to. He's calm all the way down, just like he'd been in the car earlier. He's collected and cool, a solid fixture I can rely on. He holds my hand tight and leads me with a tough composure that makes me feel secure. I don't doubt his abilities or knowledge of where we are going for a moment, and I like him being in charge. He's so protective of me.

We reach the bottom of the hill and Cove pushes back a tree branch. The leaves part and then suddenly, I see it.

A beach.

Just like Cove had said.

Totally empty.

Pristine. Untouched.

Cove's secret beach.

Wow.

So, it's actually real. And Cove's never shown this to anyone else. My heart starts beating faster at that thought.

"No one's been here since I was seventeen," Cove says, taking a step on to the white sand. The place looks like the kind of tropical paradise you'd see on a computer desktop wallpaper. Clear water, green trees, white smooth sand, and sunshine. *Literally* perfect.

This is paradise.

A week ago, I was sitting in my cramped apartment in Queens pouring over a nursing textbook, and now I'm standing on a remote beach untouched by humans for years on the other side of the world alone with a man ripped from the pages of a model catalog. How crazy's that?

I can't believe this.

"You used to come here as a teenager?" I ask the hunk of a man standing next to me.

"All the time."

"I'm jealous."

"Oh," Cove says with a wink. "You should be."

"I was surrounded by tall buildings, but you were surrounded by tall waves."

"Well," Cove replies, taking my hand and guiding me across the sand. "Now you can see how I lived."

He takes me to the edge of the sand where the beach meets the ocean. Strong waves tumble down and crash on the shore. My toes touch the cool ocean water as it drifts up to my feet. I look back to see my footprints leading from the tree line, a set of footprints right next to Cove's.

"Is the water safe to swim in?" I ask him as we look out across the roaring ocean.

He smiles at me and lets go of my hand. "As long as I'm here," he replies.

* * *

DON'T FALL OFF. *Don't fall off. Don't fall off.*

My teeth chatter from the cold. Sandy's old wetsuit clung to me, wet from the ocean. Sandy's height, much more considerable than mine, means that her wetsuit fits me like an oversized glove. So, basically, it doesn't fit me at all.

The ocean water's cold. Freezing, in fact. Thoughts of hypothermia bubbled in the back of my mind.

Don't want to freeze to death.

But the main thing I'm worried about is falling off the surfboard.

Don't fall off.

I'm lying on the board, spread out, as Cove pulls it along the surface of the water. He's in front of me, pushing through the waves.

Cove flicks his handsome head around to face me and I try to focus on his piercing blue eyes and blonde wavy hair and not on the roaring waves crashing around me.

The ocean's a scary place, and I'm bobbling along in the middle of it on a piece of fiberglass no bigger than my body.

Oh, god.

But Cove is with me, and every time he turns his head to look at me, and I see myself in his beautiful eyes, I realize I'm safe with him.

Don't fall off. Don't fall off. Don't fall off.

I cling on tight to the sides of the surfboard as Cove pulls it along. The water's at his chest height and he's having to start to paddle. It's getting deep. I don't want to think about how deep we are. I've never been in an ocean beyond my waist before, but I don't want to embarrass myself in front of Cove.

"You're doing fine," Cove says to me, obviously seeing the terrified expression on my face.

"Fine's not the most *accurate* word to describe me right now," I reply. My hands are sore from how hard I'm gripping the sides of the surfboard.

"You are fine, Miss Ripley Sailor," Cove says. He stops moving and leans his gorgeous and well-structured face towards me so that our mouths are mere inches away. "Just remember what I taught you on the beach, and you'll be more than fine."

The beach. A few minutes ago. Yeah, he *tried* to teach me how to stand on the board. He gave me a lesson on the sand on how to do it, and I *tried* to listen, but I was already so terrified of going into the water that his words filtered through my ears and out the other side without me taking any of it in.

"I don't remember anything," I say, and Cove chuckles.

"There's a chance you'll fall off," Cove tells me. I raise an eyebrow at him. "Okay, there's a *very high* chance you'll fall off. And if you do, then you're going to get dumped by a wave. This is when you get caught in its spin underwater. It sounds, and feels, scarier than it actually is. You will tumble around in the water and won't know which way is up, but don't worry, the tumble will end, and your body will naturally find its feet. All you need to do is hold your breath, and if you don't, you'll end up with half the ocean in your nose."

"Dumped by a wave? Now you tell me this?" I ask incredulously.

Cove smiles at me, flashing his white teeth, and I'm instantly calmed. His smile can do that to me. "Don't worry, you'll be fine. Just stand up and you'll be all set."

He spins the board, and me, around so that I'm facing the shoreline. I glance behind to see Cove watching an incoming wave. The thing approaching us is massive, even taller than I'd thought it'd be.

A massive, terrifying wave.

I'm terrified.

Oh, god, he's gonna push me ahead of the incoming blue wall. He's gonna let the wave carry me to the shore.

This is it.

"Start paddling, Ripley," Cove instructs as he pushes the surfboard along with the wave. He disappears behind me as the wave picks me up and shoots me forward. I feel the board surge as I'm lifted to the crest of the wave. My hands and feet flap away at the water as I attempt to paddle like the surfers I've seen in films.

I'm *doing* it. I'm on the wave speeding down towards the beach.

And now it's my time to stand up.

Cove's instructions echo in my ear as I shoot along the wave. Hands below my chest, palms flat on the board and push my body up on my feet in one quick movement, that's what I need to do.

Okay, I can do this. Cove is watching.

I get my hands into position. The surfboard rocks precariously beneath me. I steady myself and push up just like Cove has told me to.

I feel the soles of my feet touch the fiberglass board.

Yes.

And then I'm tipping over.

Oh, no.

I fall off the side of the board.

And then I'm in the water.

I tumble around the inside of the wave. Water rushes up my nose and I can't breathe.

And then I'm standing again. The wave has gone. The surfboard, its rope still tied to my foot, is bobbling next to me. I'm near the shoreline, in the shallows.

I cough and splutter. It does seem like half the ocean is caught up in my nose and mouth, just like Cove said it would be. I gag, swallowing large chunks of the saltwater.

I don't even notice Cove swimming up gracefully beside me until he's standing over me, laughing his head off.

Oh, he's finding this hilarious.

"What's so funny?" I ask through hiccups of ocean water.

Cove can't contain his laughter. "You. You're funny, Ripley."

"I *nearly* drowned, Cove."

He shakes his head. "No, you didn't."

"Did too. And if I did, you'll be charged as an accessory to murder."

"I can think of worse reasons to be locked away for," Cove says, still laughing. I can really punch his stupid, gorgeous face now. "You'll do better with practice."

I raise my eyebrows at him. "Well, at least we have every day for six months to practice," I tell him. He stops laughing then. "Unless I do drown, then you're in this for the long haul, Cove Finn. Six more months."

Oh, I do find a lot of pleasure in watching his face drop as he contemplates six more months of this.

And then it's me who is the one laughing.

15

RIPLEY

I knock on Cove's door.

Almost immediately, he opens it. Wearing just his board shorts, showing off his impressive set of abs and ripped pecs, Cove leans against his doorframe and winks at me cockily. I don't know how he can be so cool all the time, it's so effortless.

"Oh, I'm ready, Ripley," he says, flashing his perfect grin at me, and my body wants to collapse under the sheer intensity of his smile. He knows how to make me go weak at the knees with just one look.

"Just like every morning, huh?" I ask, punching his solid abs playfully. Cove doesn't even flinch.

"Just like every morning," he replies. He strolls past me towards the front door, picking up his car keys on the way out. I watch his toned ass pass me.

"I'm driving today."

"You always drive," I say, pouting.

"Exactly. It's my car."

I skip up beside him as he opens my car door for me.

"Such a gentleman," I say sarcastically. Cove rolls his eyes and sits in the driver's seat.

"You're in a playful mood today, Ripley Sailor. What's got into you?"

"I'm just excited about the beach today, that's all," I reply. "Maybe I'll stand up for the first time."

"Maybe you finally will today. I mean, it's only been *two weeks*."

"Hey!" I giggle, slapping his knee next to mine. He's teasing me and I kinda like it. "We all know you're some wannabe beach god, but surfing doesn't come as naturally to me as it does to you. Give an American girl a break."

Despite my cheekiness, I feel myself blushing at Cove's comment about my playfulness. I really *am* in a playful mood. Last night I dreamed of Cove, I dreamed of being in his bed and him wrapping his arms around me. In the dream, he was lying next to me, completely naked. And then I woke up and my pussy was wet. I can't get him out of my mind, and so seeing him in person just sets off some weird energy inside me, I can't stop.

And now, in the car, he's sensed it and it's making me blush.

Of course, I've been dreaming about Cove, of course, I have. How can't I not be when we've been spending almost all our time over the last two weeks together? We've fallen into the same routine every single day. Every morning at seven I'll go and knock at his door ready in Sandy's old wetsuit. Cove will wake and get dressed into his revealing board shorts, then he'll drive us to his secret beach where we spend all morning alone together. Him trying to teach me to surf and me trying not to fall off for the hundredth time. I haven't been able to stand yet, but I'm working hard at it.

Yeah, give an American girl a break, especially when she has to look at this Adonis every day.

"So," I ask Cove as he drives us out of Sandy's driveway and onto the main road. "What's the topic of discussion for today?"

"Hmm," Cove relaxes his hands on the steering wheel and looks out the window. Trees and houses fly past us as we shoot down the road. He only likes driving at super-fast speeds. He doesn't give a damn about the cops. "How about we talk about our favorite things?"

The two of us have gotten to know more and more about each other on our little car trips. Over time, and a *hell* of a lot of questions, I'm slowly able to break through Cove's cold playboy exterior and am really getting to understand him. He's starting to be willing to show me glimpses of who he really is underneath his bad-boy facade. It's a struggle at first; the man knows how to joke and tease and avoid any serious discussion, but I've got to slowly wear him down car trip after car trip. I think it has something to do with my impeccable charm, but it's probably more due to the fact I can be a real annoying little brat when I want to be. Whatever it is, it's worked. And now Cove and I have a close familiarity I never expected us to have on that first day we met when he stood in front of me fully naked and didn't shake my hand. We have a back-and-forth now that I've never really had with anyone else. We're getting to know each other really, really well.

And I'm beginning to like him. Like, really, really *like* him.

I can't ignore my feelings any longer. I'm starting to dream about him more often. It isn't just my physical reactions to his athletic and muscular body that are setting me off anymore, but the more I get to fully understand his personality and his real nature, the more I know I'm falling for him.

And I can't help it.

We are the most unlikely of pairings, but somehow – somehow - we just *work* together.

"Okay," I say, turning to face Cove as he drives us towards his secret beach. "What favorite things do you want to talk about?"

He shrugs. "I dunno. What's your favorite drink?"

"Easy," I reply. "A chocolate milkshake."

"Chocolate milkshakes? How old are you, like seven years old?"

"Hey, don't knock it. Chocolate milkshakes are the *best*."

"It's pretty weird for a twenty-year-old to be into them."

"No, it isn't."

Cove turns to me and smiled. "Yeah, it is."

"Not if you make them the proper way. I bet you've never made them properly."

"Okay, so what's the proper way, then?"

"Well, I used to do them with my Mom. She'd get the nicest ice cream to make them from the store. It's gotta be fresh and vanilla. Then, when you do have the nicest ice cream, you also have to make sure you have the best chocolate syrup to mix it with. And then you do it all in a blender with some milk," I say. I turn to look out the window. "Mom worked seven days a week as a nurse when I was a kid to keep a roof over our heads. The time when we got to make milkshakes together was the time when I saw my Mom be the happiest she's ever been."

Cove places his hand on my knee. "Okay, you're only going to hear this from me *one* time, but that was very sweet."

He's cute.

I continue staring out the window so that he can't see the tears in my eyes. I miss my Mom so much. I think of her going to work back home just to make sure I can go to college. That's why I need the money offered by Sandy's dad so that I can let her retire early.

That would be the best thing I could ever do for her after everything she's done for me.

"So," I say, wiping away the tears on the back of my hand. "What's your favorite drink, then?"

Cove pouts his kissable lips and sighs. "Beer, I guess."

"Beer? Why?"

"I dunno, I just like it."

"*Right.* That's not as good or as interesting as my story."

"No," he laughed. "No, it isn't."

* * *

"Take my hand," Cove says as we stand at the tree line leading down to the secret beach. He's parked the car at the same place he always does, and we will have to stumble through the thick bush all the way down to reach the beach. And, like every time, Cove offers his hand for me to grip as he leads me through the foliage. Under his other arm is his teenage surfboard I practice on.

"Trust me, Ripley Sailor."

Two weeks of going to the beach every day and Cove has yet to surf. He's not even gone on the actual surfboard once. He really doesn't want to get on the board at all. I'm sad for him, his one passion in life cut short by just one accident a year ago. I look at him, at his muscular frame, and see that the man is so *ashamed* of himself. He never wants to surf again.

He's so full of shame.

I wish he could see himself the way I see him.

I take his hand and follow him down, careful not to fall over on any of the slippery rocks or upturned roots. This is always the hardest part to reach the beach. I hate having to crawl through the bushland to get to paradise.

But I do like doing it with Cove. I do like how he always, without fail, offers his hand to help me through.

Gripping his hand and feeling his soft, but masculine, hold on mine always makes my heart soar. He makes me feel like no other girl. I bet he never did this with anyone else. I bet all those girls he's slept with never saw this side of him. He lets me into his vulnerable side, and I soak it up.

I know he's letting me see a side to him no one else sees.

Every day we're getting closer and closer. Every day I felt my heart beating faster and faster the longer I'm with him.

Cove is unlike every other man I've met, and I feel safe with him. Trusted. Secure. As he leads me down the trees to the secret beach by his hand, I feel protected, like nothing can touch me.

And I think I'm changing him. I've not seen him with another girl since that first day we went surfing. I've not smelled alcohol on his breath or seen weed in his room.

He's even washed his clothes.

Even his bedsheets.

This is all down to me.

I know he's doing all this for me.

And I love it.

We reach the secret beach, and we do what we always do. Cove takes the surfboard, dumps it on the sand, and teaches me how to stand so that I will be ready to do so in the actual ocean. All the time I can sense his wariness around the board. He still hadn't got over his aversion to surfing. He still doesn't want to surf. I wish he does. I wish he shows me what he's like when he did surf when he was in his natural element. I can only imagine it.

He takes me out on the board, pulling it, and me, along as he paddles us a few hundred yards out into the ocean. I spend the time focused on his beautiful sandy hair and the shape of his sharp jawline. His hand sometimes grazes mine and I physically shudder at the thought of us so close together.

Where once I was terrified of the open water, he's made me feel confident. Cove's confidence has rubbed off on me like it's contagious. I'm no longer scared of the ocean, especially when I'm with him.

"Ready, American girl," Cove says every time when he spots a good incoming wave on which to launch me on. I smile and nod my head, thinking that this is my chance to finally stand up.

And then, when the wave is about to go over his head, he pushes me onto it and lets me go.

Every time as I shoot down the wave, I try to stand, just wanting to impress him. I just want him to know that every day spent with me is not going to waste, that I *listen* to him. I just want him to be proud of me and of the teaching he's done.

And every time I fall off the board before I get the chance to stand up. Every. Single. Time.

This particular American girl from Queens is not made to stand up on a long piece of fiberglass in the Australian ocean.

And today is no different.

After a couple of tries in the water, we retreat back to the beach, exhausted. Cove is dripping wet. I laugh at how his bleach-blonde hair sticks to his face and I watch water droplets fall from his defined torso. He grins at me with his white straight teeth and collapses onto the sand next to me whilst I stare out at the ocean. I hear his heavy breathing just inches from me. His muscular chest rises and falls. His eyes are shut as he slowly relaxes. The sun is bright and there are no clouds in the sky. It's just us two alone on this stretch of perfect sand.

It really is paradise here. With Cove.

As I stare out at the ocean, I think I see something far out. Something black. A whole group of black dots jumping in and out of the water.

"What's that?" I ask, pointing at what I'm seeing. Cove opens his eyes and rests upon his hands to get a better view. "Are they dolphins?"

Cove laughs. "Yeah, they are."

"God, they're *amazing*."

"They really are."

"Did you used to see them when you used to surf?"

"All the time," Cove replies. "Did you know every dolphin has a unique whistle?"

"No?"

"Yeah," he says. "They can recognize former lovers' whistles even after twenty years apart."

I look at Cove. He's still staring out at the dolphins with an intense focus. "Is that true?" I ask.

"Yeah."

He stands up then to get a better view of the dolphins as they jump in and out of the water, crossing his arms.

I watch his small dolphin tattoo on his lower back, and I think only one thought. The thought that's been replaying in my head constantly on a loop these last few weeks.

Cove Finn.

I'm slowly falling in love with you.

16

COVE

Everything changed today.

The day when Ripley stood on the surfboard for the first time.

The past few weeks have been weird, like, super *weird*. Sure, I've reluctantly agreed on working with the American girl, just like my dad and Sandy have wanted, purely so that I can be guaranteed the money I'm owed, but then things have gradually changed until everything's changed. Until today.

Instead of just merely going through the motions of spending time with Ripley Sailor, I'm beginning to *actually* like her. We're actually becoming friends, even despite my best intentions.

I'm beginning to like her? What the hell?

I think it started when I punched that prick, James, in that parking lot the first day Ripley and I spent together. The words he called her that day, the way he dismissively glanced at her up and down like she was nothing but my cheap accessory. He made me so furious in that moment that I resorted to my monkey side and aggressively took him down. I just had to. He insulted Ripley, and, honestly, only I can do that.

I was protecting her.

I must admit, punching him in his dumb face was pretty *damn* satisfying. Hearing the crack of my fist against his nose made me feel strong in a primate sense, like I was a knight protecting a damsel.

And the look on Ripley's face straight afterward, that cute mixture of awe and surprise she had, was just the perfect cherry on top of the cake. She was worth it, punching that prick in public. I didn't give a shit about him calling the police because she was worth any punishment coming my way.

And from that moment on, I know we'd get along well.

But I didn't know I would actually start liking the girl.

That all changed today. The day she finally stood on that surfboard.

We've been spending every morning together for the past few weeks, every day consisting of me teaching her surfing at my secret beach and her trying to stand on my teenage board.

I didn't know why, at first, I showed her the secret beach, but I soon realized that I did so because I trusted her. She isn't like anyone else I know in town, and I know she won't run around telling people about me. She isn't here with me for the attention and reputation of being with New Water's most eligible and bad boy bachelor. She's just here to help me.

I think she's pretty goddamn cute.

Contrary to my first impression, Ripley's not just some annoying American girl coming here with her loud accent to disrupt my life. I mean, sure, she did disrupt my life - because of her I've had to begrudgingly scrub the drugs and drink and girls clean from my life, but after the initial first few days of strong withdrawal symptoms - especially for the girls - I don't miss my vices at all, being clean and alone with Ripley has made up for all those temptations.

Jesus, Cove, are you actually going soft for the girl?

Maybe I am.

Damn.

Who knew all it'll take would be some geeky American girl to melt the cold heart of a billionaire playboy surfer?

Well, Ripley's melting my cold heart.

I've actually *liked* waking up early with Ripley knocking at my door, ready to take her surfing. I've *liked* driving her to my secret beach. I've *liked* taking her hand and guiding her down the bushland to the sand.

I've *liked* teaching her to surf.

Ripley, despite not being my type at all, is exactly the girl for me.

I've been so entrenched in my views that no one will ever like me, especially not since the accident, I've never actually given time to the thought that maybe *someone* actually would like me, that maybe someone will find something to like within me. I never thought that to be a possibility.

But Ripley does.

Ripley likes me.

I can tell.

She laughs at my jokes, and I see her staring at me in the moments she thinks I'm not looking. She trusts me when I teach her to surf in the ocean. I know she's terrified of the ocean, yet she's put that aside and has trusted me to look after her. I can't believe it.

She actually trusts me.

Plus, she does look cute on the surfboard in that wetsuit.

I've noticed she has a pair of great tits under that wetsuit that she's kept hidden from the world.

And she has a world-class ass.

Trust me, as a connoisseur of good tits and asses I would know; I've had a few myself. And she has an absolutely *banging* body. If only she were more confident in revealing it, but that's what I like about her.

She isn't just some preppy American girl or one of the fake chicks pursuing me in Tide, she's a *beauty*, inside and out. I can't believe it's taken me showing her how to surf for me to realize that.

I'm such an idiot.

And things didn't seem different at the beginning of today, the day when Ripley first stood on the surfboard. But everything soon changed.

This morning she knocked on my door at exactly seven on-the-dot, the same time she always has done for the last two weeks. We got in the car as normal and I drove her to the secret beach, chatting about the most stupid topics together as we always have done. *God*, she makes me laugh so much sometimes with her silly jokes and funny observations, she's a real queen of comedy.

We drove up to the secret beach, and I guided her down the bush to the sand, as I always have done. And then we went out surfing. I pulled the board out through the water with her on it. We waited for the perfect wave and, when it eventually came, I pushed the board on it. She shot down the wave towards the shore with me watching on from the ocean, just as we've always have done.

I saw her placing her hands in position under her chest. I saw her lifting her body. I saw her pushing her legs up so that she's standing on the board.

And, for the first time, she's up on the board.

My heart leaps in my chest.

"I'm standing, Cove!" she yells back at me as she surfs the wave. "I'm standing!"

I immediately start swimming back towards the shore, back towards her.

She's only been standing on the boarding for only a few seconds before she falls off, but, still, she's actually done it. Finally. She's *surfing*.

I reach her. Ripley's wiping back her wet hair, smiling and laughing. So am I.

I can't believe it. I've taught her to surf.

She squeals in joy and wraps her arms around me, excited at what's happened.

Her face buries in my chest. We hug.

She disentangles her face from my body and looks up at me. Our lips are only an inch apart.

She's so fucking beautiful.

And then we kiss.

And everything changes.

It happens so naturally, so spontaneously that it takes me a moment to register what we're doing, that we are actually kissing.

A deep, passionate kiss.

Her lips fit perfectly around mine. I bite her lip and she responds by pressing her mouth stronger against mine.

Out of all the kisses I've had in my life, with all the models and girls at Tide, this one ranks as number one. By far.

I feel her tongue on mine. Her lips taste sweet and also salty from the ocean water. She's soft. My hands raise around to her back and she melts into my arms.

She's mine, and I'm hers.

It's perfect.

It was always meant to be.

And now here we are, standing in the shallows of the ocean, on our own secret beach. Kissing.

It's the best kiss I've ever had.

And then Ripley pulls back. She lifts her lips away from mine and twists her body away.

"I... I can't do this, Cove," she stammers, her voice softly breaking.

No. Wait.

I can't believe it.

The kiss felt right. This is *right*. Why, then, is she breaking away from me?

"Why can't you?" I ask. The panic builds in my chest.

She lowers her head so that I can no longer see her face. "Because of the deal I made with your dad and your sister," she whispers, and I can tell she's hurting inside, that this is tearing her up. Because of me. "Because you're *you*, and I'm me. Because of your sister. Because of who you are. You're a womanizer. Because of *everything*."

No. This can't be happening.

The kiss was perfect.

She can't be rejecting me.

I'm silent. I can't move. Everything's shattering around me. The ocean water splashes around my ankles, cold. Eventually, I take in a deep breath and I reach out under her chin, bringing her head up to face me to see into her eyes. Her upset eyes. She looks at me with a look that can ruin me. She doesn't want to say the things she's saying, but I know that, deep within her, they are the truth. She's saying her truth.

She's made a deal with my family, and now she's broken it. And now she's tearing up inside.

I stare deep into her eyes and whisper. "Did you want to kiss me?"

It's the only question that I need answering. I want to know. I *need* to know.

"Yes," she replies tenderly.

That's all I need. Screw everything else.

"See?"

"But, Cove, there's too much to think about. There was a deal I made."

"What else is there to think about?" I ask. "Forget about my dad, or my sister, or who I've been, and look at the man who's standing in front of you right here and right now. This is all that matters."

I wish she can see this for what it is.

No deal's coming between me and the most perfect kiss I've ever experienced.

Ripley shakes her head and slowly removes my hand from her chin. I can sense she's already growing distant from me.

Distant from me, just like everyone else has done since the accident. I've seen that look before, that look of pity that people love to give me when they see me on the street or when they see my scars.

It's the same look that makes me want to crawl under my bedsheets and die. I've just never expected to see it coming from my American girl.

"I don't want to talk about it anymore," Ripley says. "I don't want to surf anymore today. I think the lesson's over. Let's just go home."

And that's it. She's walking away from me back towards the bush to the car with the surfboard under her arm.

No. Wait.

No girl has ever rejected my romantic advances since my heartless supermodel girlfriend dumped me during surgery.

But this is different.

This American girl is doing something to me. By rejecting me, she's harming me in ways no other person can. She doesn't know it, but she has my whole heart in her hands and now she's squeezing it. Leaving it out to dry. And I'm in pain.

Why did I let her in?

Why did I let her see the real me?

I should've known she'll hurt me. I should've known she'll ruin me.

I chase after her, but she doesn't talk. We don't speak even on the car journey home.

It's all gone horribly wrong.

Ripley is quiet and distant from me.

And I know I have to fix this.

17

COVE

I RAISE my fist to knock at Ripley's door, but I hesitate. I take in a deep breath and still I can't do it. I can't knock on her door.

What the hell, Cove?

But no matter how much I try, I can't bring myself to knock on her bedroom door.

I actually can't do this.

I know why. It can't be, but for the first time in a long time, I'm actually nervous.

I'm scared of her opening the door. I'm actually nervous about seeing Ripley again.

This is serious. I've never, ever been like this and especially not with a *girl*. I'm the infamous billionaire playboy, Cove Finn; nervousness shouldn't be in my vocabulary, especially when it comes to women.

But here I am. Nervous.

The infamous billionaire playboy reduced to blubbering in front of a geeky American girl.

What would the clubbers at Tide think of me if they saw me now?

This all comes down to one thing.

The kiss.

That perfect kiss Ripley and I had shared on our secret beach.

Ripley was right at the beach about the deal she made with my dad and Sandy; it can't, and *shouldn't*, be broken, especially by a kiss. No matter how romantic and perfect it seemed. I kissed her when I shouldn't have, and it's jeopardized her trust with my family. That forbidden kiss has broken the terms of the contract she made with Sandy and my dad.

I don't give a fuck if it has, but clearly, Ripley does, and she's the most important person in my life right now.

So, it's down to me now. I have to fix this.

I have to make amends.

But the kiss was perfect. She knows it. I know it.

But the kiss was wrong.

And I have to fix this.

I raise my fist again, ready to knock on her door.

This is hard.

It's midday. It's been a few hours since we wordlessly returned from the secret beach. We haven't spoken or even seen each other since Ripley ran through the front door and into her room the minute I parked the car outside the house. I was left standing, alone, in the middle of Sandy's kitchen, not knowing what to do. I know I shouldn't let some American girl tear my heart out, but yet she's still affecting me hours after she broke off our kiss. My past playboy self would've laughed if he'd knew I'd let a girl influence my emotions, but that's what kissing Ripley Sailor has done to me.

I'm as lost and as confused as she is.

This has never happened to me. I'm never confused, especially over a girl.

What is happening to me?

I have to make things right for the better.

Outside her bedroom door, I take in another deep breath.

Fuck it. Here goes.

Finally summoning up the courage, I knock on Ripley's door. I hear her scrambling around the room before she opens it. A scramble of panic and nerves.

And there she is. Standing in her doorway.

Ripley Sailor.

She's showered and changed since she came back in her wetsuit. Now she's wearing jeans and a loose-fitting hoodie. Casual. I like it. The look suited her well. To be honest, she can look good in anything.

My breath's taken away when I see her. God, my opinion of her has changed so drastically since I first met her naked in the living room. I can see her properly now, as she deserves to be seen. She's attractive, so *fucking* attractive, and she's also so freaking cool. And smart.

In short, she's my perfect woman.

And now I've made her upset. Now I've done something wrong, something that I'm afraid will ruin our friendship forever. For the first time in nearly a year, I feel remorse for something, and it's all to do with Ripley Sailor.

Fuck.

"Hey," I say when she opens the door. I keep my gaze firmly on hers and not on her round breasts perking up through her hoodie, despite the massive temptation.

She's so cute I can lift her up right now to my lips and kiss her again.

No, Cove Finn. Don't think that. It'll only make things worse.

I see the hesitation in her eyes as she stands in her doorway, but I also see her desire lurking underneath. The desire I tried to kiss earlier that day, the desire she knows she can never give in to, the same desire I have that's flowing through my veins and makes me want to lean down and kiss her slightly opened lips right now.

Her hesitation comes from her nerves, and the raging thoughts in her head. The same conflicting thoughts I'm having as well over how right that kiss was, and how wrong it was at the same time. She doesn't know why I'm here, standing outside her door, so she's even more nervous than I am. And that's saying a lot.

"Hey," she replies, stuttering a little. She's trying to pretend she's cool and composed, that nothing is amiss, but she's trying a *bit* too hard, and I see straight through it.

"I'm getting hungry, so I think we can make some seafood together," I say. I hope my plan works. "Sandy says that you like seafood."

"Yeah, she told me you like fish and chips as well."

I nod. "I do. You hungry now? I bought some prawns, so I was thinking we could make some garlic butter to put them in if that's okay with you. And I also got some fresh vanilla ice cream and chocolate syrup and some milk, which means we can make some chocolate milkshakes, the same way you and your Mom used to make them. How about that?"

For a while, she just stares back at me, no expression on her face. I'm worried about what she's thinking. I hope this plan will work and that it will fix things between us, but the thought enters the back of my mind that maybe I've blown it yet again.

That maybe she'll reject me.

That maybe, once again, she'll break my heart like she did earlier today on the beach.

But, after some thinking, her face lights up and Ripley Sailor smiles. My insides burn up in response.

She's so fucking sexy when she's happy, and I want to make her happy every day of her life.

"Yes," she says.

And, with her affirmation, I know I've fixed it.

18

Okay, sure, to be fair, Cove can make a pretty damn good milkshake. It's nothing like the way Mom used to make them, but he's still pretty damn good, regardless.

And he's fun. He knows how to make me laugh.

He's irresistible.

"This is gonna be the weirdest combination of food ever," I giggle as Cove finishes mixing the milkshake ingredients in the blender. He takes off the lid to check inside. The drink is all milky and frothy and dark with the chocolate syrup.

Perfect.

"What's gonna be the weirdest combination of food ever?" Cove asks, mockingly mimicking my American accent.

"Prawns and chocolate milkshakes. It's super weird."

He smiles at me, pouring the contents of the blender into two tall glasses. "What? Are you saying you've never had milkshakes and prawns before? It's a traditional recipe where I come from."

Yeah, he really knows how to make me laugh, the bastard.

I know he's joking, and I laugh along with him. We cheer with our milkshake glasses and then I chug it down.

"Yeah," I say after I finish my big gulp of the chocolate drink. "That's a pretty damn good milkshake."

Cove laughs again and points at my lip.

"What?" I ask.

"You have a..."

"What?"

Cove shakes his head. "You have a chocolate milkshake mustache."

"Oh," He's right. Before I even get the chance to do so, Cove's already leaning over to wipe the frothy line from my top lip.

Oh, gosh, his finger is on my skin.

His tender touch on my lip thrills me inside like birds are fluttering anxiously around my stomach. His warm touch makes my whole body shiver with excitement.

His touch on my lip makes me remember this morning.

And his touch reminds me of that kiss we shared.

The kiss I'll never forget.

His kiss this morning was so... *unexpected*. But it was *so* welcome. It just happened, but when it did, I never wanted it to end. Our lips matched perfectly at that moment, and it was like we're made for each other, like we're two pieces of a jigsaw puzzle finally slotting into place after years of being apart.

On our secret beach this morning, I never wanted that kiss to end. I finally understand that weeks of getting closer and closer together have inevitably led to that moment. Looking back, it was inevitable that we should've kissed like that when we'd gotten as close as we had.

But I also knew I had to end it. I also knew I had to be the one to stop what we were doing.

Even though his taste was everything I want. Everything I need.

But it had to stop.

And it all came down to Sandy.

She'd told me explicitly not to get with Cove. She warned me about him, and specifically about his playboy nature. I can't just kiss Cove when I know what she'll think about us together and what she told me explicitly not to do.

Don't fuck Cove.

That's what she said.

She's my best friend and going around her back like that was wrong; I had to put an end to it as soon as it started.

No matter how gorgeous her brother is, or how right his touch feels.

I don't want to reject Cove, but I have to think with my head.

Drinking from our milkshakes, Cove and I start preparing the prawns and garlic butter.

He's bought all the right ingredients. I watch him work, his big arms delicately opening the packaging, his intense focus on the garlic butter, the way he carefully handles the food.

What a tender man underneath all the bravado.

The way he cooks, he makes my heart swoon, and I begin to realize that he'd bought all this food to impress me, as a way to make up for the kiss, and as a way to apologize in a way he only knows how. How sweet. How caring. He really does think about me, he really doesn't want to lose me.

Why, Ripley? Why do you fall in love with the one man you shouldn't?

This is hard.

So hard.

I don't know how my heart can handle this; my soul is torn between two extremes. Cove and Sandy. Between the most beautiful man I've ever met and my best friend.

It's a choice I never want to make.

We finish making the butter, our hands soaked in the stuff. My fingers are coated in the gooey liquid.

"We're absolutely covered in butter," I giggle.

Cove flicks some towards me and I scream in terror. "You're the messy one," he says with a laugh.

"No, you are!"

"You are!"

We run the kitchen tap and wash the butter off our hands, playfully pushing each other all the while.

We laugh and fake fight until our bodies are touching and our hands are holding on to each other. Our faces are close. Our fighting pace slows, and we look at each other in the eye. Cove's intense stare pierces through me and my heartbeat crawls to a stop.

He's so close. He's so present. He's so near my heart.

"Hey, Ripley," he says softly, nearly whispering. His fingers tighten around mine. I don't fight back; I'm enjoying his touch way too much.

"Yeah?"

"About that kiss."

"Yeah?"

"What do you think about it?"

I flick my hair back, and I don't know what to say. I'm torn in so many ways, but the way Cove is looking at me with his bright blue eyes... I just... can't resist him.

"I'm worried about Sandy finding out," I reply sadly. "I'm scared of what'd happen if she finds out, and I'm scared about losing you in my life."

"You don't have to be scared, Ripley."

"I just want to keep it a secret."

Cove leans in with his face so that our lips are nearly touching. "I'm not good at keeping secrets," he says. His soft Australian accent makes my throat dry up and I melt in his voice. "Everyone in this small town seems to know everything about me, apparently, and I don't care. I don't care about everyone knowing about us, even my sister."

I know I can just fall into temptation right here and now, but I have to be strong, even with Cove Finn. I can't let my feelings rush to my head. I can't let them take over and dictate what I do, no matter how much I want to. "I have to remind you that everything is on the line, Cove. The money. Your money. My place at nursing university. Your inheritance. Everything is riding on this."

Cove doesn't seem affected by my excuses. It's like he sees through my defenses and into what I truly feel. He sees my endless desire for him and he's unfazed by the excuses I've built around myself. I can't handle him anymore. He's too strong for me; I can't resist him for much longer.

I can't contain my body for much longer.

"Ripley," he whispers. "Answer me one thing. Was the kiss wrong or not?"

He knows my answer.

"It wasn't wrong..." I pause. Our faces are *so* close. I've stopped breathing. My heart is ready to burst out of my chest. Cove is all-encompassing me; he's my world and I see nothing but him. He's cast a spell on me with his strong physicality and his confident presence, and I can do nothing to defend my natural inclinations from him. Nothing I can do can stop my heart from falling for him. "It felt right?"

Cove smiles and our lips grazed each other. I *can* kiss him, I just can. It's what I want. My whole body is screaming *yes*.

Do it.

It's what I need to do.

"Yeah, Ripley Sailor," Cove says just before our lips touch. "Trust me, it felt right."

And then, for the second time that day, we're kissing.

Kissing.

No. Listen to your heart, Ripley.

I break free from the kiss and Cove continues staring at me, expression indecipherable.

I can't give in this easily.

"What about your sister?" I ask. I'm so weak for him; one more word from him and I'll be gone, placed completely under his spell. Does he not know the power he has over me with just the sweet sound of his voice? The delicate touch of his finger on my lip? He has me utterly under his control. He must know that. "I'm so worried about her finding out about this. About us,"

Cove, still unfazed by my questioning, speaks quickly, as if he's been thinking of this sentence all morning, and maybe he has. "What does your heart tell you?"

My heart tells me that this is right. So unbelievable, irresistible, gloriously right.

Yes.

That's what my heart tells me.

And that's it.

He has me totally under his control. Hook, line, and sinker.

Our lips fall upon each other's once again, and this time I lose all my defenses. I can't stop my heart now even if I try. Cove has me utterly under his spell. He has my lips. He has my body.

He has my heart.

It's the best kiss. It's the right kiss.

It's so taboo, but it's so right.

This is what my heart wants.

And then Cove has his arms around me. He completely surrounds me. He's my everything. He has me in his arms and then he's picking me up. He holds me close to him, my feet up in the air like I weigh nothing. His muscles are against my chest and his thick arms around my entire body.

He's carrying me. Our lips are still locked passionately, but he's carrying me across the kitchen, across the open-plan living room, and straight into his bedroom. I don't struggle against his grasp. I don't say no. I know exactly where he's taking me, and my body is screaming yes.

I know where he's taking me, and I want this.

Oh God, the man can kiss.

In no time at all, we're in his bedroom, the same room where, just two weeks ago, I was nagging him to clean up. The place is spotless now and the bedsheets are fresh, the result of my hard work convincing Cove to clean up his act. Just like its owner, the room has changed completely in two weeks and has shown me its true side.

Cove delicately places me down on his bed, but I don't care about where I am anymore. Instead, I'm completely focused on his lips on mine. The way he kisses me, the way he bites my lip, the way he hungers for my touch sends me wild and over the edge.

I'm wet for Cove Finn.

Cove breaks the kiss, and he stands over me as I lie on the bed. The way he looks at me with that arousal glinting in his blue eyes makes me feel so sexy.

He wants me.

I see the large bulge in his pants. I can't believe how turned on he is; it's like an animal has taken over him, a ravenous and hungry animal, thirsting for me.

And me alone.

I can't believe it. *This* is what my body does to him. I can't help thinking of that perfect naked body of his I saw on the first day we met. That toned athletic and muscular body is now turned on because of *me*.

"Ripley," he whispers with all the confidence of a man who gets anything he wants. "I'm going to fuck you."

I gasp involuntarily at his strong words. My sex is on fire just by looking at him and hearing his rough accent say those words. I try to swallow the lump in my throat.

"*Yes*, please," is all I can manage to say in return. A wave of excitement passes through me.

I know he's a bad man, and that he's going to do nasty things to me.

And I want it.

Cove, still standing over me, tears off his shirt. My breath catches in my throat as I see his ripped abs flex and the V shape of muscles that disappear into his pants. I lean up from the bed and eagerly rip down his jeans.

There he is.

His cock is so large, even bigger than what I remember from our first meeting. It hangs between his legs. Heavily.

A well-endowed, beautiful man.

A man who is focused entirely on me.

Oh, God. He is ready to fuck me.

I don't know how I'll be able to handle him and his massive member. But I'm gonna try.

He grabs my hips and throws me back onto the bed, tearing down my own jeans. I slide out of my hoodie so that I'm entirely naked in front of him.

"I'm ready for you, Ripley," he mutters, voice breathy with bursting desire.

I'm not a virgin, but I haven't been naked in front of anyone for so long, and yet I don't feel uncomfortable or self-conscious in front of Cove. By the way he looks at me, Cove just makes me feel so goddamn *sexy*. All my worries fly out the window.

He reaches down with his hand and he tenderly touches my sex with his fingers. I shudder when I feel him. His blue eyes flicker with an intense arousal as I gasp yet again. He leans down and ravenously sucks on my nipple between his teeth as he slides his fingers into me. My eyes go wide with wild desire as I feel him inside of me.

Oh, god. Yes.

His fingers reach deep within me and my back arches off the bed. He rides me hard with his hand. Pumping me. Controlling my body with just a flick of his finger inside me. I jerk in pleasure as waves of delight crash within my body, spreading all the way up from my hot pussy.

Don't stop, please don't stop.

I look down at him. His blue ocean eyes are full of triumph and it's so *hot*. He's so hot.

He brings his gorgeous face down past my tits and towards the middle of my spread legs. I let off another involuntary gasp from my mouth as his tongue grazes my clit. Warmth floods up from my wet sex.

The man knows how to pleasure me, that's for sure. He drives me wild.

His tongue plays with my clit as I hear the rustling sound of a condom packet being opened.

"Please, Cove," I moan. "I want you inside me right now."

I just can't wait. I need him.

I want him now.

Cove's tongue lifts off my clit, and then, in one graceful move, he enters me.

His massive cock penetrates me with a force that makes me go cross-eyed.

He pushes himself into me, my pussy wet and welcoming for his member. He slides in, moaning, as I finally lose all sense of control. A giant wave of pleasure rocks my very core, and my mind is dominated by one single thought that spurs me to orgasm.

Cove Finn is inside me.

With a hand on the bed to steady himself, Cove begins to pump me. His cock thrusts deep inside me like he really is a wild animal, his pure desperation and animalistic greed for me making me blush. I want him, I want him so bad. Sweat pours off him, drenching me in his fluid with every thrust.

I *love* it.

I love seeing his ferocious desire manifest as he continues to fuck me.

And he fucks me *hard*.

"You're so beautiful," Cove whispers, and my heart melts. I let him kiss me. My hands run through his perfectly tousled blonde hair. I can *feel* him. Every part of him.

He's mine, and I'm his.

This is paradise.

"Speak for yourself," I reply, barely able to breathe through my gasps of delight. "You're so beautiful, Cove."

My body rocks harder and harder as it reaches its climax, I'm moaning as I feel Cove's cock pump deeper and deeper inside me with every thrust. I'm going to cum.

I'm going to-

And it happens. My heart seems to stop. I lose all my senses as pleasure seeps into every corner of my body. My legs jerk and Cove grunts as his cock twitches inside me.

Wow.

We'd both reached climax together.

19

RIPLEY

I'M LYING next to Cove Finn. I, Ripley Sailor, am lying next to Cove *freaking* Finn in his bed. I can't believe it.

A few weeks ago, we hated each other's guts, and now he's sleeping with me. He's snoring peacefully next to me in his giant bed.

Cove Finn is sleeping next to me.

We'd fallen into a deep sleep after our round of debauched fucking, and now it seems like I'm the first to wake.

I turn to face the sleeping body of Cove and then I don't dare move a muscle. I realize I don't want to wake him; I just want to watch him doze away in that sweet way he's currently doing. The cocky beast is still at last.

He's sleeping next to me.

His body's so vulnerable and so tranquil, lying there in his fresh silk sheets. My heart is ready to burst just watching him doze, watching his chest rise and fall quietly.

I'm lying in bed next to Cove *freaking* Finn.

I reach my hand out to rest on his chest. I just want to feel him, I just want to touch his inviting body. His skin is warm.

This is a dream, but I'm living it.

As my hand lies on his firm chest, Cove's eyes blink slowly open. His attention turns to me lying next to him. My heart skips a beat as his blue eyes rest on mine, his stare penetrating into my soul.

"Hello, American girl," he coos softly.

"Hello," I whisper back, not daring to break the quiet tension between us.

"Have I been asleep?"

"Yeah."

"You've been very naughty, you've made me tired," he says, and I blush. Color seeps into my cheeks as I hear his tough accent tenderly accuse me in a playful way. I like it.

"You don't exactly give me an easy time either," I reply.

"Oh, but it's fun."

"Is it?"

His eyes flick off mine and scans down the length of my naked body, taking it all in. "Oh, yes. The best fun I've had in a long time."

Damn.

My breathing stops when I hear that. I think of all the girls he must've had over his playboy days, and now he's telling me I've been the best fun in a long time? Hope runs through my veins with the optimistic thought that I'm different from all the girls who've come before. I'm special in Cove's eyes. He doesn't know how those words affect me, or how they made me feel.

Can this moment get any more magical?

I ruffle my hand through his blonde hair. He's all salty from the ocean and so evenly tanned from a lifetime under the Australian sun. He's my golden boy. My surfer.

My lover.

"Well, that was also a lot of fun for me," I say, and it's true, my body has not even begun to recover from the sex session we'd just had. My pussy is still soaking wet and my body is radiating with that pleasurable after-sex glow. With just his two fingers and a delicate touch, he's made me feel things I've never felt before.

"Yeah, I can clearly see you enjoyed that, Ripley Sailor."

So, I'm not hiding it that well.

I'll probably won't walk straight for a week after what he's done to me.

I brush my head up against his shoulder and Cove wraps his arm around me. I snuggle in against his hot, muscular chest that rises and falls with his breathing. I can hear his steady, slow heartbeat like a rhythm in my ear. I'm safe. I'm protected. This man has me in his strong arms. I try to blow away a strand of my brown hair that falls over my nose and Cove laughs at my pathetic little attempt.

I'm not like one of his other girls. I've changed him, and he's changed me. For one thing, I can now stand on a surfboard, and I hadn't even been in a proper ocean until a few weeks ago.

Maybe, if he'd gone this far, *maybe* I can get him to get back on the board. Maybe I can encourage him to surf again.

That'll be ideal.

"Tell me something," I say, smirking.

"What, Ripley Sailor?"

"Your tattoo, the one of a dolphin. I've constantly been seeing it. What does it mean? Why did you get it?"

Cove breathes in. I know he's thinking. I know he doesn't really like talking about himself, especially his inner thoughts and emotions. I know he never speaks like this to anyone else. He trusts me like I trust him. "They're my favorite animal," he replies softly, like he's telling me a secret. It is a secret. His secret.

I know I'm being let into some information he rarely divulges to anyone. He's no longer the carefree bad boy of New Water in my eyes. Instead, he's Cove Finn to me, my surfing teacher. The man who held my hand and guided me to a secret beach that only he and I know of.

"Your favorite animal? Why?"

"They're free, I guess. They're free in the ocean, and plus, they're smart. They just get to ride the waves. That doesn't sound like such a bad life to me."

This is my chance to press him, to find out more about him. I've been wanting to unpeel his protective layers for so long and now, finally, he's opening up to me. "Is that what you would want to do forever? Ride the waves?"

Cove sighs and runs his hand through my hair. My head tingles as he carefully massages my scalp. "I only wish I could. It's just... these scars make things difficult."

"Yeah."

"They're so hard to live with, and they were so painful during the surgeries. They're just a permanent reminder of my failure every day I look at them. I don't think I'll ever surf again. You saw how James treated me. I'll be laughed out of every beach in the Southern Hemisphere, and that's something Dad and Sandy don't understand. They don't see the faces of the people I grew up surfing with when I see them. They don't see the pity and the snide remarks I have to see. I'll never show my face at a populated beach ever again. So, no, you won't see me standing on a surfboard anytime soon."

My heart just crumbles at hearing him speak like that.

"You shouldn't say those things," I reply. "They're not true."

I wish he could see what I see. What I see of him.

"But they *are* true, Ripley. I hate that accident and I hate these scars."

I know he's going to say that he hates himself, but he bites his tongue.

So much shame inside him. So much pain.

Cove Finn portrays himself as a reckless playboy to the outside world, but inside, he's hurting like a little boy. It's his only defense but, with me, it crumbles completely. I see right through him. I see the little boy who's hurting.

We don't speak a word. I hold his body closer and I feel his arm tighten around me. We stay, cuddling, for the next hour in his bed until Sandy's scheduled to come home from work.

* * *

Mom's soft voice echoes down my phone. Hearing her familiar voice immediately calms me. It's good to hear her again. I'm immediately transported to our little kitchen table back in Queens like it's one of our late-night conversations.

"Hello, sweetheart," Mom says when I call. Sandy's just arrived back from work and I greeted her at the front door, pretending that nothing's amiss. Pretending that I hadn't just fucked her brother in his bedroom. And now I'm back in my own room.

I want to talk to Mom, so I'm happy she almost immediately picks up when I ring her phone.

"Hi, Mom. How are you today?"

"You know me, same old."

I imagine her waking up for another day working at the hospital as a nurse. All the years of her working her butt off in that place just to keep me in school, all those years raising me whilst working full time. The woman is a saint.

She's my anchor.

I just want to make sure she never has to work again. If I can hold out here for a few more months and get the money from Sandy's dad, then Mom will never have to step into a hospital as a nurse ever again.

That's all I want.

I think about my dad and how he'd walked out on her when she needed him the most. That experience has scarred her for life, and it also scarred me. All men are like that.

Cove is a man, so he's also like that.

No, Ripley. Don't think like that about Cove.

But I know, deep down, it's true. All it will take is for a man I care about, like Cove, to walk out of my life to scar me in the same way Dad permanently scarred Mom.

I can't trust men when I've seen what happened to Mom.

"You're doing okay?" I ask her down the phone.

"I'm doing fine, sweetheart. Don't you dare worry about me. Focus on your life down there. How's everything?"

I want to tell her everything. I want to tell her about Cove and me, but I hold my tongue. I want to tell her about the new hope I'm having, the hope I've felt this afternoon when Cove kissed me for the second time. The second kiss. The tender way he spoke to me, the way that made me feel like the only girl in the world. The way he held me in his strong, manly arms. I want to let her know about the chaos my heart is feeling around this surfer boy and the uncontrollable way he makes me feel every time he glances at me with those deep blue eyes. I want to divulge everything to her like I'm a giddy schoolgirl. I want to tell her how *right* this all feels.

I want to tell her *everything*, but I hold back.

I don't want to overwhelm her. I don't want to give her

false hope. I don't want to explain everything just for my heart to be broken by this billionaire playboy.

I don't want to be scarred by a man just like Mom was.

"I'm fine, Mom. There's nothing new to report. I'm just living my best life down here."

"That's great. Is Sandy looking after you well? How is she?"

"She's great, Mom. Just great."

"And you're going to the beach every day? I wish I could see it."

I smile, tears coming to my eyes.

I just miss my Mom. I wish she were here; I wish I could tell her everything.

"Every day, Mom. I'm going to the beach every day. It's just the best. I know you'd love it if you saw it."

"Oh, Ripley."

"I love you, Mom," I say. My throat's caught, and I'm beginning to cry. "I miss you so much, Mom."

She pauses. She knows I'm crying, and she knows something's bothering me. She knows me too well to know when I'm upset. But she doesn't mention my crying. She just asks me the best thing she can ask me right now. She becomes my mother and calms me down with one request.

"Tell me about the beach, Ripley," she asks. "Tell me everything about the beach."

And, crying down the phone, I tell my Mom everything about the beach.

20

COVE

THE BEACH USED to be my safe space before the accident. The place I can go to in order to escape and meditate on my problems.

But that was before I fell off my board in that fucking surf competition a year ago. Before that fateful day, I could walk along the beach alone in my thoughts and just be myself. But that was before the accident, before I swore off surfing forever.

The beach was always somewhere I could go to hide from the world, to let my mind recover and regroup. To think.

The beach was somewhere I could go to rediscover myself.

I've avoided the beach like bats avoid the sun. I've never wanted to step foot on sand ever again, not until Ripley Sailor flew into my life and forced me to teach her surfing. For the last year, until that American girl swanned into New Water, I never wanted to hear the pleasant sound of waves crashing on the shore ever again. I never wanted to walk alone along a beach ever again.

But now, after making love with Ripley Sailor, I can walk alone along the public beach once more. Wrapped in my own thoughts, rediscovering myself.

I'm back on the main beach of New Water.

What's happened to me over the last few weeks? I've been molded. Shaped beyond all recognition.

Is this all the American girl's doing? Is she the one who gave me the spark of courage to walk along the beach once more? It can't be.

Surely, I've not been changed by a girl. The billionaire playboy Cove Finn, transformed by a girl?

Could I have really allowed someone to enter my life and transform me in the way Ripley *fucking* Sailor has done so quickly?

Dammit, this American girl has got a hold over me, and I don't think I can escape.

As I walk barefoot across the beach, the wet sand soft under my toes, I come to the conclusion that yes, I really have allowed Ripley Sailor to come into my life and change it for the better.

No way, but it's true.

Gone are the drinks, drugs, and girls. All that's left is just me and Ripley.

Everything in my life has changed in just a few weeks. All thanks to one person.

I turn my head towards the roaring ocean crashing on the sand yards away from me and look out over the view. Surfers dance far out in the distance along waves you'd only see in a place as beautiful and as wild as Australia. After a year of recovery and avoidance of this very place - the beach - I am finally able to watch surfers do their thing with unbridled joy written on my face.

Ripley Sailor's changed me. For the better.

I'm happy to be here, on the sand once more. I no longer care if someone I know from my surfer past, like that James prick, sees me here. I no longer care about their looks of sympathy or their snide remarks when they see the scars on my legs and recognize the infamous surfing failure with the bad boy reputation. They can say anything they want to me and my mind will just turn to thoughts of Ripley Sailor tightly wrapped around me in my bed.

Ripley Sailor is all I need.

Forget about all those other girls who came before - all those fake girls from Tide or the international supermodels or the legions of girls who relentlessly pursued the most eligible bachelor in New Water - none of them could ever match up to this geeky American girl and the way she looks at me. Or the way she talks to me. Or the way she smiles at me. Or the way she melts my cold heart.

She means *everything* to me.

But she's *too* kind, she's *too* caring. I know, as a hundred percent fact, that I don't deserve her in my life.

She's too good for me.

And the hardest part is that she's giving her love to me unconditionally. She's done so much for me in the last few weeks, things way above what my dad has paid her to do. She's utterly stripped away my layers and totally exposed my innermost self. A side of me even I haven't seen before.

I'm a better person because of Ripley Sailor.

I don't deserve an angel like her to fly into my life.

I lean over and scoop up a handful of sand. This beach. This is my land. This is my home.

In a reversal of what I say to her every day before I lead her by my hand down to the secret beach... I *trust* her. She's the one who pulled me from the brink.

And I don't deserve her.

21

RIPLEY

Before he pushes me into the wave, Cove leans over the surfboard right up to my face and gives me a long kiss. Our tongues meet, my mouth openly inviting him in. And then he pulls back. And there's a reason why he does so. I peek up to see the incoming wave behind him heading straight for us. He knew it was coming.

Cove winks at me, his masculine, unending confidence shining in his bright blue eyes.

Curse this gorgeous man and his grip over my fluttering heart.

"Good luck," he says, pushing me, and the board, directly into the path of the wall of blue water.

I'm pulled by the wave, skimming along the crest of the water towards the shore. As the board begins to scarily tilt forward, I angle my hands below my chest and push myself up just as Cove has taught me a million times on the sand. My feet find anchor on top of the board, and then, as the board clips along the surface of the wave, I'm standing up.

I'm on top of the surfboard, speeding down the wave.

I'm *surfing*.

I whoop and yell in joy, hearing Cove's cries of encouragement and celebration far behind me. I'm making him proud.

I owe this all to him, my handsome surfer.

I face away from my unbearably sexy surfing teacher and towards the shore, soaring towards it at a super-fast pace on top of the wave, the longest time I've spent standing on the board. I'm all focus. Determination. I'm going to make it to the shore this time without falling off.

So, this is surfing. Not just standing up, but *proper* full-on Kelly-Slater-in-Hawaii surfing.

It feels more like flying.

No wonder most of Australia is addicted to this sport all day long. No wonder why Aussies spent their whole lives at the beach just doing this over and over. In and out of the waves.

This is intoxicating, this is addictive.

This is the best feeling in the world.

Just what Cove likes to tell me. I gotta admit it's true.

I end up at the shoreline still balancing on top of the surfboard. I've made it without falling off. A *massive* victory. Cove has really taught me well.

My sexy surfing teacher is by my side in moments. He's swum up back to the beach, his powerful arms making long strides in the water to catch up to me in time for me to hop off the board and stroll back to the beach.

He grabs me in his arms and lifts me off the sand, twirling me around in the air, his smile shining brightly in the afternoon sun. I know I've made him so proud. After the year he's had, I'm happy to make him happy.

That adorable smile of his melts my soul every time.

"You did it," he says, lifting me higher so that I feel like I can touch the clear sky, a sky as blue as Cove's eyes.

"We did it together," I scream, excited, in reply.

I really don't believe it. He's done this. We've done this.

Cove brings me back down to his level and I feel his thick biceps push into me as he holds me close to his body. His eyes burn deep in me. "I am *so* proud of you, American girl."

I boop his perfect nose in delight. "I had a pretty good teacher," I reply.

Cove bites his full lip. "And will you say you've had a pretty... *sexy* teacher?" Oh, he wants me, I can tell.

Also, he's got a raging hard-on. That helps.

Pretty naughty of him when we're on our secret beach, alone. Who knows what can happen?

"Yeah, my teacher looks alright," I tease as I reach down to rub his solid abs. Boy, do I love his muscles. "But he can do with more abs, though. He's not muscular enough for my liking."

He likes it when I tease him.

Cove pouts at me and starts to sprint, with me in his arms, away from the water and towards the cliffs of the beach. He carries me with such ease. It's like I'm lighter than a surfboard to him. I love his strength. His physical abilities.

And, oh, he's so horny.

I know that look he's giving me. I've seen it from him plenty of times, that animalistic desire that spreads across his face.

He wants to fuck me.

"This not muscular enough for you?" he asks, still carrying me and sprinting towards the cliffs. When we reach them, he gently lowers me to the sandy ground. He wraps himself around so that he's on top of me and I'm facing him, completely trapped in by his thick muscular arms. *Yummy.*

I love that I can't escape from him. I don't want to.

"Unfortunately, I'll need a bit more of a demonstration," I reply playfully. I'll say anything to see his cute little pout again.

Keep teasing him, make his sexual anticipation build until he can't do anything but ravish you.

That's what I want, and I know he wants it too.

"I'm not going to fuck you, if that's what you're asking," Cove says devilishly, winking at me.

What? He can't say that.

He lets his big strong grip on me go and stands up.

"Cove!" I cry out. "Don't leave, that's not fair."

"You're all horny now?" he asks.

I pout and answer in a childish high pitch. "Yes."

Come back to me.

God, I hate that man. He's such a *tease.* He's got me all sexually fired up for nothing, and he knows it.

"You want a demonstration of my muscular prowess?" he asks with his dead-gorgeous smile on his face.

And before I can answer he turns around and runs off towards the ocean, his sprinting flicking up dust clouds of sand behind him as he heads straight for the water. I watch him disappear further and further away, my pussy raging with unfulfilled tension. His body is like an athletic machine, all toned muscle. He's a billionaire surfing god, and he's chosen me to be his girl. My poor heart can't stand it.

It's too much for me to take.

Yeah, I think I'm *falling* for him. That's definite.

But, as I sit on that secret beach and watch the man of my dreams sprint away towards the water, I'm still worried. I'm not an idiot or naïve, I know what men are like.

Men like my dad.

I know, deep down, that I can't trust Cove. I know he could tear apart my heart with his own hands if he so wanted to, and I'll have no defense against him breaking my heart. All he has to do to break my heart forever is to just walk away from me, for him to just grow tired of what this geeky American girl can offer him. Grow bored with me. Men are like that. Men are like my dad.

They're womanizers.

And Cove, with his storied history and bad-boy reputation, is the biggest womanizer of them all.

It's only a matter of time before he runs away, before he returns to Tide, before he runs to the pussy of a prettier and richer girl than you, Ripley.

Cove turns back and waves enthusiastically at me when he reaches the water. I wave back, subdued. My thoughts are a dark cloud shadowing this precious moment, but I know they're right. I continue watching Cove as he sprints into the ocean, diving in under a wave in a bid to impress me. I shake my head and laugh, but inside I'm freaking out.

I shouldn't forget Sandy.

Sandy.

What if she found out about Cove and me? What'll happen then? How would she react if she found out about us?

Not her.

I don't want to lie, and especially not to my best friend. The person who'd done so much for me, the person who let me live at their house for months and months rent and expenses free. She deserves better than that.

She's my best friend in the whole wide world, and I'm *sleeping* with her brother after she's explicitly forbidden it. I'm an asshole. I'm the bad guy here. I'm directly contravening the terms of the deal I have made with her and her dad.

Damn.

I will have to tell her. The secret will have to come out somehow.

But as I sit on our secret beach and watch the surfer boy swim effortlessly in the ocean, diving under the waves and flicking water off his bleach-blonde hair, I tell myself that he hasn't been doing what I've imagined at all. There's been no sign he'll leave me, despite his womanizing past. In the weeks we've been together, he hasn't been running off to the nightclub and I haven't seen evidence of weed around his bedroom. The man is *clean*. Maybe he is changing. Maybe I am changing him. Maybe Sandy has been right in choosing me to do this. It seems like I'm doing a better job than the most expensive and elite physiologists in Australia, apparently.

Maybe I am good for him.

Maybe I have been overthinking the link between men and my dad and Cove. Maybe it is possible they aren't all alike.

Maybe Cove will never leave me.

Maybe he won't.

He emerges from the water; a dripping, near-naked man full of pure animal sex. My hormones fire off without warning as he strolls towards me. He moves with total conviction and determination towards me, towards his prize.

And my body is gladly here for him to use.

Here is a man who knows what he wants, and he's going to get it no matter what stands in his way.

I'm what he wants.

I lean back in the soft warm sand, allowing the X-rated, sexually charged fantasies of Cove I've kept locked away to come to the forefront of my mind, replacing every doubt I have about him. My whole body screams out in excited ecstasy as he approaches. I can't control myself even if I do try.

I'm so ready for him and for his body.

My pussy's wet and welcoming as every part of my body lights on fire. As he gets nearer, I look up to see his serious face. He's focused, totally devoted, on me. Such precision. Such desire.

And I know one thing. One thing that I do know for sure.

This man is coming to fuck me.

And I want it.

22

COVE

I FUCK Ripley hard on our secret beach, just the way she asks me to. In amongst the sand and the crashing waves behind us, we fuck in a place we know no other people except for us have ever been.

It's so fucking sexy.

Only Ripley and I have wandered on this patch of earth. Our own secret beach is our own secret love nest. We fuck under the hot Australia sun with me still freshly dripping wet from the ocean water, and when we kiss on the sand, we both taste of the salt of the sea. It is natural and pure and raw.

It's the best fuck I've ever had.

And we go hard at it.

The woman's a sexual goddess. She melts in my embrace as I thrust into her, and I *love* that. She gives me permission to be in total control, to take full responsibility for her pleasure, and it's fucking glorious. Sexy. It's not a responsibility I take lightly. I eagerly use my fingers and drive deep inside her wet, inviting sex, tenderly touching her in a way that makes her luscious body shake with uncontrolled joy.

I'm in control of her pleasure. I'm the one who makes her groan when and where I want her to.

It's a responsibility I don't take for granted. That I work extra hard at.

I revel in her unsuppressed moans as my fingers dig deeper. I curl them inside her and feel how she responds to my touch. Her rising moans of pleasure and ecstasy make my erection rock hard as I'm turned on more and more with every thrust of my fingers into her warm pussy. We stare deep into each other's eyes as I gladly make her writhe in delight with just the flick of my finger on her engorged clit.

Shake for me, darling. Shake for me.

She is totally, completely, utterly under my control.

And I *love* it.

"I'm aching for you, Cove," she whispers between groans as my fingers flick inside her. "I'm aching all over for your massive dick."

"Don't worry," I reply with a smile on my face. Ripley leans up to hungrily bite my lip as she groans again. "I'm going to give it to you."

Oh, I am.

I've snuck in a condom down to the secret beach in preparation for this moment. When I know she can't take any more of my fingers and simply wants my cock to force inside her, I slip the condom onto my hard dick, and, with one thrust, I enter Ripley.

Yes.

Her eyes go wild, and she murmurs such a sexual and climatic gasp that fires me up. I can't restrain myself.

I want her. I want all of her.

This is where I'm supposed to be. Inside her.

Her hands dart across my body as I fuck her hard. She's reaching out for me, grabbing at me all over. It's rough. Wild. Exciting.

And I'm in control.

She squeals as I pump away and it's hard not to cum as she stares at me with such powerful longing in her beautiful brown eyes.

I lean over her, our mouths almost touching. I'm teasing her, teaching her a lesson like how I've been teaching her surfing. Our lips lightly touch. Her mouth's wet and her breath's hot.

"*Please,*" she whispers.

She's begging me. Begging me to fuck her even harder. Begging me to kiss her.

"Stay quiet, girl, and let my cock do all the talking."

She leans up and bites my lip again, begging me to kiss her. And so I do. Our lips seal in a passionate lock. She kisses me like she's possessed, like her hunger can't be satiated without devouring me whole. I fuck her hard and we kiss even harder.

I want her. I want all of her.

And then, in one mighty moment, I reach orgasm. I come. Ripley shrieks as my body tenses.

Oh, fuck yes.

"Fuck, Ripley."

She holds me close, her hot breathing against my ear and her hands ruffling up my hair, as I pour into her. She purrs as I come, enjoying it as much as I am.

Yeah, that's the best fucking sex I've ever had.

On our own secret beach. With no one else around.

It's so sexy.

Just us and the waves and the sand and the salt and the sun.

* * *

RIPLEY DOESN'T WANT to untangle herself from me, and it's kinda cute. It's cute the way she's wrapped herself around me, refusing to let go even as she slowly drifts off to sleep.

We lie on the sand on our secret beach, blissful after our amazing fuck fest earlier this afternoon. I'm still sore from it and I know I can't even begin to understand what Ripley must be feeling if I'm still stiff from it. But, judging from the warm way she's cuddling me, she *loved* it very much.

I watch the American girl as she falls asleep. I hold her in my arms protectively as her eyelids get progressively heavier and heavier and she finds it harder to stay awake. It's cute, but I'm stuck. Her own limbs aren't going to let go of my body easily.

Oops.

I really am stuck, but I don't care. This is heaven.

I can't believe she wants to care for me like this. I can't get my head around the fact she wants to be here with me. She actually *wants* me. She's so different from anyone I've ever met.

This strange geeky American girl has flown into my home from a distant country and has worn me down with her funny accent and her sassy attitude. She's absolutely nothing like the other girls I've encountered who passionately fall at my feet like adoring fans. Ripley makes me work for it. Work for *her*. Those other girls who just see me as this rich bad boy they can kiss and tell on - run to a tabloid - they don't care about me as Ripley does, they're only after my famous billionaire name and my notorious reputation and the money from an interview deal. *WHAT'S IT LIKE IN COVE FINN'S BED.* All that crap.

But Ripley Sailor doesn't see me like that. She sees me

for who I really am. She cares for me, not for my reputation or my name, but for *me*.

And I know how rare that kind of care is, and I also know that, when and if you find it in life, you have to hold on to it tight. You may never find a love as rare as this again. Some people never do.

With everything stripped away, including my name, wealth, and reputation, it all just boils down to one thing. It all boils down to one dynamic between us.

I am her surfer boy, and she is my American girl.

And I don't deserve any of this.

I don't deserve *her*.

She's absolutely perfect in every way. And I don't deserve her.

She's like a miracle entering my life the way she has. The way we've found each other.

I was the one who fell off that surfboard. I was the one, because of my mistake a year ago, to end up in hospital. I was the one who fell into the twisted self-destructive spiral of drugs and drink and girls and fucked my whole life up. I, out of anyone, don't deserve a second chance, and I especially don't deserve Ripley Sailor.

And Ripley Sailor doesn't deserve to get hurt by me.

Because she will. Because I'm me and she's her. I'm the big bad wolf. I will ruin her somehow.

She needs someone better than me. She *deserves* that.

I tenderly kiss her forehead as she sleeps. She stirs at my touch, softly purring and adjusting her arm across my chest to hold me tighter before she drifts back off.

Damn. This is too perfect.

This angel deserves someone better than me.

23

RIPLEY

ANOTHER DAY, another surfing lesson from Cove at our secret beach.

"I'm doing it again!" I scream as I surf down another wave. Cove watches me from further out in the ocean, his dazzling smile able to be spotted even from where I am.

I really am doing it again and again. Surfing, that is. This lesson I'm actually managing to get standing on the board more and more and longer and longer with each try. My feet easily find the fiberglass board and my balance is improving with every wave I surf. There are fewer times where I'll awkwardly tumble off the board and into the water. Slowly, and with more practice, surfing is becoming second nature to me.

In short, I am becoming a surfer.

Just like Cove.

Me.

Ripley Sailor.

The girl with the super pale complexion from all the way in Queens is becoming a surfer.

I'm even developing a tan.

What the hell?

I bet my accent will be next to change. Soon I'll get that Aussie twang. Give it a month and I'll be a full-on Australian.

And you'll never know I'm from Queens.

And Cove, every day, is getting prouder of me.

That's the best thing of all.

These have been the best few weeks of my life, without a doubt. Waking up every day, knocking on Cove's door, driving with him, making our way to the secret beach, our surf lessons, making love on the sand and in his bed. Everything's just *perfect*. This has been paradise. A dream.

And I know it's too late to do anything for my heart. I can't change anything now.

I have totally fallen for Cove Finn.

The billionaire playboy surfer. We're the most unlikely pairing.

And the craziest thing is that he's fallen for me too.

Yeah, like I've said, a dream.

After today's surf lesson, Cove tackles me playfully in the surf. The waves wash over us as he kisses me passionately on the sand.

It's just us on our secret beach.

The salt's in his hair and his wet naked torso presses against mine as the ocean laps at our knees. The hot sun beats down heavily on our backs as Cove pulls me in tighter to kiss me. I melt into his arms and he holds me close. The water's cold, but his body is warm.

This is where I should be.

I break free from his addictive grip on me as if I'm reaching for air.

Cove dominates my every waking and sleeping thought like a welcome intruder. I want him near me every moment of every day.

"How about you try it?" I ask under my breath. Cove hears me even with the roaring waves crashing around us.

He glares at me in confusion. He doesn't know what I mean or what I'm trying to say. "Me? Try what?"

"You know," I reply. This is delicate. I have to be delicate. I don't want to upset my man. "Surfing. How about you try surfing again?"

Come on, Cove. Please say yes.

"No."

I expected that.

It's a hard no, but I want to persist. This is my chance to change his mind.

Maybe he will change his mind for me.

I keep talking, convincing myself that I can convince Cove. "We're on a secret beach. There's no one else here to see you around here for miles and miles. It's just me, standing here in front of you. Just my two eyes and no one else. You know me. You trust me."

"I do trust you."

"Then," I say, resting my hand on his muscular pecs. "How about you just try to surf, just once, and see if you can still do it? This is your best chance to try it. The best chance."

Cove turns his head away from me and I know I am losing him, but I want him to at least *try*.

I want to see him surf.

"Please, Cove."

"No, Ripley."

"This is the best time and place for you to try to do it. Just stand up on the board. That's all you need to do, just like I've been doing. Like how you've taught me. That's easy for you. Please just stand up once and see what it's like again. It'll feel great, I promise."

Cove sighs and turns back to face me, and that's when I get to see the pain behind his eyes, the pain he always tries so desperately to hide from everyone, even me. "I can't, Ripley."

His voice is soft and distant.

"Why not?" I ask. I try not to be, but I'm growing more and more frustrated with him and his non-commitment. It's not my place to make him do something he doesn't want to do, but surfing has been his whole life. He always speaks of it as being his passion, and now he's just going to block off from doing it ever again for the rest of his life? Just because of one stupid accident? He isn't even going to try at least once? That's not a great way to live. "Why can't you, Cove?"

Please say yes.

Cove looks me deep in the eyes and he speaks slowly. Great sadness and shame choke his voice. "Because I'm scared, Ripley."

Oh.

At that moment, he is the most vulnerable I've ever seen him be. This is who he is underneath all that bravado and cockiness and bad boy attitude. I can see him now. He's just a scared, scarred boy, afraid of failing again.

But I won't let him fail again.

"I'll be here. Do it for me," I say softly. "Please."

Cove pauses. He watches me carefully, like he's trying to read me like a book. I see the tumult unfolding within him. His mind. All the different thoughts and ideas and hope and fears clashing against each other in one big mess. He's thinking.

"I'll fall off again."

He is so scared.

"No, you won't," I say, pressing harder. "You're a natural at this. What happened at the surf competition a year ago was no fault of yours. It was just an accident."

"I will. I'll fall off again."

"No, you're Cove Finn, the best amateur surfer in the Southern Hemisphere," I say with a smile. I need to break through to him; I need to make him understand. I know he does somewhere inside. He just needs a push from someone he loves. Someone like me. "Don't you want to be that again? You've said surfing is the best feeling in the world. Don't you want to feel that again?"

He nods slowly. "I do," he says.

"Then do it for me. This is your best chance at doing it again, so what are you waiting for?"

Is he coming around to the idea? Am I convincing him? I think I am.

"I'll do it for you," he replies.

My heart leaps in my chest.

Yes.

"You will?"

Cove nods. His mind is made up. "I will."

He's doing this for me.

I can't believe it. This is major. He, the guy who's said he'll never surf again, is going to get back on the surfboard and get back into the water. I will actually be able to watch my man do what he does best.

And it's because I've asked him. He's doing this for me.

My heart dissolves. I take his hands in mine and feel his warm body.

He's doing this for me.

* * *

THE WATER DRIFTS UP to my toes on the sand as I wait on the shoreline, my finger dangling nervously in my mouth. I'm biting my fingernail, watching Cove and his perfect body head out into the ocean with the surfboard he'd practiced on as a teenager under his arm. His board shorts are riding low in the way that only his board shorts seem to do, revealing just enough of his ass to make my body involuntarily shudder.

Cove's going to surf for me. Because I've asked him to.

He's doing this for me.

He's fast in the water. To get over a wave, he leaps on the board and starts to paddle. This was a move he's practiced hundreds of times, thousands of times before. This was what he does best. And, of course, I know there's a little bit of him showing off to me, but that's more than fine. I like to watch him show off to me. I like his cocky attitude.

I like to watch him when he's sexy and passionate. When he's like this.

He calmly waits in the water for a good wave. When one does come, Cove spins his board around and swims with it, catching the wave smoothly.

This is it. This is when he'll stand. My heart's in my throat. My nerves are on edge.

He's going to surf again.

And then he's standing on the board.

Yes.

He's getting up.

He's doing it. He's really doing it.

And then, as soon as he gets up, he falls.

No.

He falls off the surfboard.

I watch on in shock as his body tumbles into the water like he's a lifeless doll.

And then he's gone under the surface of the ocean. The wave's swallowed him up.

24

RIPLEY

I HAVE to pull Cove from the water. He's conscious, but weak, his eyes fluttering as he recovers from the shock of the fall. His body's soft and delicate as I pull him from the surface of the water. Nothing like the normal Cove I'm used to.

He was struggling to stand up when I found him in the ocean.

A moment earlier he was standing on his teenage surf-board, victorious, and now he's not even able to swim.

Please be okay.

I didn't even have time to react to him falling off his board when I rushed into the water to help him.

I take him out from the waves, wrapping his arm around my shoulders, lifting him up, and helping him limp out of the shallows and onto the safe sand of the beach. His weight is heavy on me as he staggers out of the rough ocean.

He's hurt.

"It's okay," he says between shallow breaths as we

stumble back to the beach. "I can do this on my own, Ripley. Let me go."

His voice is weak and tired. He can barely breathe.

I know he can't actually walk on his own. Despite what he says, he can barely stand by himself, let alone use his legs. He's still recovering from the shock of that fall. I have to help him, but his arrogant pride is trying to get in the way. He needs my help, but he's not prepared to ask for it.

Typical Cove.

We reach the sand.

We've made it out of the ocean.

We're okay.

Cove tries wriggling out from my hold the moment our feet are no longer in the water and I try to stop him, knowing he'll only fall if he tries to walk on his own.

He's too full of pride to let me carry him.

"You're hurt," I say as he attempts to get away from me and stand on his own.

"Stop carrying me, Ripley. I'm okay. I can do this by myself." Cove's voice is full of bubbling anger.

Anger at me.

Anger that I'm the one carrying him out of the water.

Anger at me for helping him.

Fine then, have it your way.

I'm not doing this if he's going to bark at me like that.

I let go of him and he stumbles onto the sand. He doesn't want to show weakness in front of me, no matter what, no matter how much I'm trying to help him. Can't he see it's me here trying to help? No one else? Can't he trust me?

I'll do anything for you, Cove. Anything.

"You're hurt, Cove. Maybe I should call an ambulance."

"Don't," he commands sternly. He looks up at me with

his blue eyes, his face full of nothing but anger. "Don't call an ambulance, Ripley. I'm fine."

"You sure?"

Cove goes quiet. "You made me go into the water," he says with an undertone of menace.

What?

"No, I didn't make you go into the water," I reply. I can't believe what I was hearing. He's blaming me for this?

"You did. You made me."

"No, I *asked* you to try surfing for me," I say. "I didn't force you to do anything you didn't want to do."

Cove's not backing down. "You knew what I felt about surfing. You knew how I never wanted to do it again, but you asked me to do it for you. You knew I can't refuse your wishes, Ripley. I can't refuse your wishes. I couldn't. You knew that I can't refuse but still you asked me to surf and then I fell off, just as I predicted. And it's all because of you."

"So, you're blaming me?"

I don't believe this.

He *is* blaming me.

His voice gets louder now. Full of spite and anger. "I told you this would happen, that this was exactly I was scared of and yet you still persuaded me to get into the fucking water. It's your fault, Ripley." He points down at his trembling legs. His scars are so visible, it's like they're shining in the sun. "This was all your fault."

No.

"Hang on, I just asked you to try. I didn't force you."

Cove shakes his head, his breathing slowing. He looks away from me at the sand, his face snarling. "This was all a big mistake."

"What was?" I ask, tears forming in my eyes.

No, don't cry, Ripley. Not now. Not in front of Cove.

"It was all a big mistake."

"What was a mistake?"

"All of this," he says, gesturing at the whole beach, but it's like he's gesturing at everything - our last few weeks together, our *time* spent together. Our time falling in love. He's saying it was all a mistake. "You trusted me and pushed me to surf and then I fucking failed again. The exact same thing happened as what happened in the surf competition. I fell off again. I fucking failed, again."

"You didn't fail," I try to say, but Cove cuts me off with an aggressive wave of his hand.

"You've taken everything away from me, everything I liked, everything I used to cope with my pain." He's in his own world, his own train of thought. He's growing angrier with each poisonous word that escapes his lips. This is the Cove I saw that first day I met him. This is the arrogant Cove. The selfish *asshole*. This is the Cove who was distant from me and mocking of me the day we met. He reminds me of how worlds apart we really are from each other. *The billionaire surfer boy and the pale geek from Queens.* We were never meant to meet, never meant to cross oceans to fall in love. I feel so small and it's like the Cove I love is disappearing in front of me and that there's no way I can hold on to him. "You took everything away from me, and for what? To make me surf again, to fall off again? To make me fail again? Haven't you embarrassed me enough, Ripley?"

"I haven't," I cry, and I can't stop the tears now. They come pouring out from me.

"You took away the only things that helped me cope with the scars. You took away the drugs and the nightclub, the booze, and the girls. It's all your fault."

"No, Cove." There's nothing I can say or plead with him; he's completely in his own world now, blaming me for everything. I can't reach him; my voice can't get through the anger surrounding him. Cove has changed in front of my eyes. The fall just then has woken the beast inside and I see nothing in his eyes but resentment towards me.

He's blaming me for everything. He's pushing me away.

It's everything I feared coming true right in front of me.

"I'm nothing but a failure. Can't you see that, Ripley? No, you can't. You could never see that. You've just been so infatuated with me that you were blind to who I really am from day one. You haven't been able to see who I am at all. I'm nothing but a failure, so why do you insist that you can fix me? I can't be fixed, Ripley. I'm not some patient to be fixed. I'm nothing but a fucking failure, but you never saw that."

He's not a failure. He's my Cove.

But he's not anymore.

He thinks I'm delusional.

He thinks he's a failure.

Cove stands then. He's unsteady on his feet, but he still manages to stand upright. I rush over to grab him in case he falls again, but he pushes me away. I don't know what to do. I'm left shaking, crying.

This man no longer wants me.

He's so, so angry at me.

Cove blames me.

I continue watching him as he crouches down and picks up his surfboard. Then, in one painful motion, he swings it away towards the cliffs of the beach. The fiberglass board bounces into the soft sand far away from us with a sad thud.

It's like he's throwing away his life. His future. Our future.

Cove immediately begins to storm away, limping towards the bush away from the beach.

Away from me.

He no longer cares about me.

"Where are you going?" I softly ask him, afraid of the answer.

Cove turns around then, his face a snarl.

He's no longer my Cove.

He's no longer that surfer boy I fell in love with. It's like the last few weeks have never happened, that they're just a wild fantasy concocted in my head. A stupid fantasy dreamed up by a stupid American geek, about a handsome Australian surfer who could never truly love her. A stupid dream, nothing more.

He throws something in the air towards me, something small. It loudly jangles as I catch it in my hands.

His car keys.

"You do whatever you want," he tells me flatly. "I'm off to get high and drunk. Life would be better if you weren't here anymore, so just *fuck off* back to America."

No.

Fuck off back to America?

Without waiting for my response, Cove turns around and stumbles off towards the trees.

I'm left standing there on our secret beach, completely destroyed as Cove disappears.

I'm left here, crying.

25

RIPLEY

Cove's gone, and he has left me all alone.

He has left me alone on the secret beach, just me and my thoughts and his car keys dangling in my useless hands as I stand here shaking in the aftermath of his fury.

Cove has gone, and I am left completely and utterly alone.

I fall down on the soft sand and continue to cry even after he's disappeared into the bush. Tears pour down my cheeks and drip onto the warm sand as the crashing of the ocean waves fills my ears. Along this long untouched beach, I sit, alone.

Without Cove.

The man has run away, exactly as my dad had done all those years ago. When it got tough, Cove has run away from me just as I'd feared he would. Cove Finn isn't special, he's just like every other guy.

I saw this coming, but I did nothing to stop it. I didn't

put up any defenses around my heart and now I'm deeply wounded.

I could follow him, I could run and find him amongst the weed and alcohol and pull him away from those vices, but that would be making the same mistake my Mom made all those years ago. I can't spend the rest of my life ruined by one man's awful decision to run away just like my Mom has done. But that life isn't for me, I'm not going to do that, I've promised myself I won't do that.

I wipe the tears from my face with the back of my hand. Sand has got in my eyes, irritating me.

I know it's time. Time to talk to Sandy about all this. It's time to open up to her. I was wrong to think I could change Cove or to hide our relationship from his sister. My best friend deserves to hear the truth from my mouth.

Sitting here on the sand, I resolve it's time to come clean to Sandy.

It's time to go home.

I follow the familiar trail up through the bush, the same trail that Cove and I have traversed so many times in the last few weeks, back up to his parked car by the road. I unlock the vehicle and sit inside, taking in a deep breath to steady myself.

Calm down, Ripley. Crying won't get you anywhere. Cove's gone.

I'm still in shock. I don't know what to do with myself. I don't want to drive. I don't want to do anything. Cove has run away, and I am left all alone with an empty void in my heart. There's nothing I want to do except be back home with Mom in our little apartment. I just want to see her again. I miss her so much after all this time apart.

I just want to feel her hug again.

Sitting inside the car, I take out my phone and dial

Sandy's number. It rings for a long time. She's at work at the school, so I doubt she'll pick up.

Please do.

After three rings, she does.

"Hello, Ripley?"

Her voice. Her lovely voice.

"Hi, Sandy," I say, holding back tears. "We need to talk."

She's quick to answer. "Where are you?"

"At a beach."

My best friend hears the emotion in my voice, my failed restraint, and instantly knows something is wrong. "Okay, go home and I'll drop everything here. I'll come home."

In the car, I shake my head. "You don't have to do that," I say.

"Of course, I do. Get home. I'm coming. When I get back, let's talk."

* * *

SANDY'S HOME even before I am. She opens the front door when I pull Cove's car up on the driveway, hugging me quickly before leading me inside to the kitchen table. This time there is no wine on the table. It's just us two, ready to talk.

"Tell me," she says as we sit at the table. I must look a mess. I've been crying all the way in the car back to her house. She sees how my eyes are red and wet, handing me a pack of tissues to dry them.

The whole way back to her house I've been crying over Cove and what he said to me. The final words he said to me ringing in my ears.

Life would be better if you weren't here anymore, so just fuck off back to America.

That's what he said to me before he disappeared off to his drugs and drinks. Those final words of his have burned into my soul like I've been branded with them. On the long lonely drive to Sandy's house, his voice has repeated those words over and over in my mind, slowly wearing me down, each repeat of those words slowly eroding my weak heart.

Cove has gone. You knew he'd run away from you.

"It's a long story," I say to my best friend as she sits and listens.

"I've got the time," she replies. "Tell me everything."

There's no point holding anything back now, no point in hiding any more secrets from Sandy.

Sitting at that kitchen table with Sandy, I explain everything to her. Everything that has happened between Cove and me since we met. Well... maybe not *everything* - not the *sex* parts. She doesn't need to know about those, but she gets the gist.

"At first I hated him," I say. "But then everything started to change."

I tell her about how we'd gone from enemies to lovers and how we both stripped away our defenses and each got to see the real us.

I told her how I'd fallen for him.

How I've fallen in love with Cove Finn.

And I end on his final words to me on our secret beach. His anger. I told her how he'd ran away and left me on that beach, and that's where she finds me now crying in front of her.

A broken woman.

She might as well hear the whole truth.

Sandy listens to it all, not speaking a word. She watches me intensely as I recount how I fell in love with her brother and how he's run away from me, as all men do. There are no more secrets; the load has finally been lifted from my shoulders.

And when I finish telling Sandy everything, she doesn't say anything for a long time. I'm surprised by that. Instead of screaming or yelling at me as I expect, she instead sighs and sits still, contemplating, across the table from me, clearly taking the time to think of what to say. I'm so nervous my legs are shaking underneath the table. I can't tell what she's thinking; her face is unreadable.

Have I gone too far? Have I destroyed the relationships of both my best friend and the man I love in one afternoon?

"And what do you want to do now?" she asks me quietly. She isn't angry, or yelling, or furious like I'd expected. She remains calm. Sandy isn't revealing what she really thinks about it all.

"I think I want to go home," I reply. It's the truth.

I just want to see my Mom.

"Is that what you really want to do?"

"Yes," I say, and Sandy slowly nods. She is handling this so emotionally well. God, I love her and her solid presence. "I don't trust men and I knew I shouldn't have trusted Cove. No offense."

Sandy smiles. "Oh, he's a prick and you're free to say it."

"Yeah?"

"You know, I thought something would happen between the two of you, but I didn't think he'd hurt you like this. I'm sorry that he broke your heart. Truly."

She's apologizing to me?

"I'm sorry too. For everything."

Sandy reaches over and grabs my hand tenderly. "Don't be sorry, Ripley," she says, squeezing my fingers.

"You're not angry?"

She shakes her head. "What would be the point?" she asks.

"You have every right to be. I kept this secret from you."

"Well, of course, it wasn't good that you kept it hidden from me, but you could've always have spoken to me about it. I'm your best friend, Ripley. I could never be truly angry at you. I've always been there for you and I wish you'd spoken to me sooner about all this, but I'm glad you're opening up now. I'm just sorry about my prick of a brother."

"I am so sorry."

"It's okay," she replies. "I've been there myself."

"You have?"

"Yeah. I thought I loved a guy in high school, but he turned out to be a shit as well. I hope I never see him again, so I know how you feel. Men are real dicks."

"Yeah, they are."

She smiles. "Oh, yes. They are."

"I love you, Sandy."

"I love you too, Ripley," she says. "So, what do you really want to do now?"

"I just want to go home."

"Of course," she replies. "I understand. Come, I'll drive you to the airport now. There's a flight that leaves for Sydney in a few hours and there you can transfer onto one to New York."

"Thank you, Sandy. For everything."

I truly mean it.

"Okay, let's pack your things and get out of here."

26

COVE

I REACH over the booth table to take the joint from Kev before relaxing back into the leather seat, taking a long drag on the weed.

This is what I need.

"What do you think?" Kev asks me, practically shouting to be heard over the thudding music of the busy nightclub. Tide's really kicking off tonight.

"Yeah, it's good," I reply as I lean back and try to let the familiar taste of the weed relax me.

Fuck me, it's been a long time since I've had one of these.

The music's loud. The nightclub's packed out. Busy and fun.

This is the life.

Here I am again. Back in Tide, back where I should be.

But something is off. Being here doesn't feel completely right.

I'm sitting in my usual VIP booth, surrounded by the normal gang of girls and my stoned drug dealer that I've not seen since Ripley came to town. So many shot glasses are arranged out on the booth table in front of me. Bottles of alcohol ready to be consumed are waiting to be poured. Everything is prepared for the beginnings of a good night.

Except it all felt odd; it's like something is missing. I've never had that feeling before in here, in Tide.

This is strange.

"Hey, Cove," the girl sitting next to me purrs, leaning into my body. Her manicured hands slowly reach down over my abs and dangerously towards my pants, her sultry voice aimed right in my ear. "I've missed you."

Is she someone I've already slept with? I don't remember. I don't even know her name and I don't even care.

I should be aroused by her wandering hands; I should be enjoying this like I'd done so many times in the past year.

But something is missing.

And I know what it is.

Ripley.

Ugh, fuck her.

But I can't get the American girl out of my head, no matter how many girls cozy up to me in this club or how many joints I smoke. I know I should be feeling better than I did about running away from her, but I'm not. I can't get over her.

That whole fucking incident at the beach. The argument.

She'd made me confused back there. Her face at the beach when she encouraged me to get back on the surfboard, my heart just melted for her right then and there. She convinced me to do something I never wanted to do again - *surf* - with just an expression on her face. And I knew that I was in love with her right then. That look she gave me to get me on that board made me fall in love with her right there on the spot.

Fuck.

Ripley Sailor is what's missing.

At our secret beach, she trusted me so completely to not fall off that board and yet I still did. I was pathetic. I failed her just as I failed everyone else a year ago.

Getting out of the water, I couldn't bear to look at her. The way she had to *help* me out of the ocean was just humiliating. When she pulled me from the water, I saw in her the same expression I'd received from everyone for the last year. That same old expression. That expression of pity. That expression of sympathy. That look at a failure.

And it was me - I was the failure. I'd fucked up in front of Ripley and she *saw it all happen*. I saw how she looked at me when she pulled me from the water.

There was no going back from that, no reversing how she felt or what she saw.

Me falling off the board.

Again.

In front of her.

What a fucking failure you are, Cove.

She decided to open up too much to me and what did she get? She got Cove Finn falling on his first attempt. Typical me. A fuck-up.

She trusted me not to hurt her, and yet I still did. I heard her crying when I left her on the beach.

She had the wild thought that she could fix me. Who did she think she was?

I hurt her.

I hurt the best love I'd ever known. I've failed and I've hurt her.

And that's what's stinging the most.

I don't care about this club, or the people - or even the girls - inside it. I haven't given any of them a second glance.

I only care about Ripley *fucking* Sailor.

"How about shots, Cove? Let's do some shots!" With

the excited shriek of one of the girls in the VIP booth, I'm alerted back into the room. Another girl was on my other side, rubbing my hair. So, I had a girl on both sides of me, practically begging for my cock. The other girls in the booth are currently opening the bottle of vodka, pouring it into shot glasses. Another girl bounces up and down in excitement, her giant fake tits bouncing along as well. Another girl's winking at me from across the booth, sucking on her finger seductively as she scans my athletic body up and down.

I should be happy. This should make me happy. It certainly would've, back in the time before that American girl flew into my life.

But now I have a hole in my heart that can't be filled by drugs or drinks or girls.

None of this means anything to me anymore.

Wow. Jesus.

I've come to the realization that nothing in this club means anything to me anymore.

Nothing.

The girls, the club, and the drugs are useless now. Empty. Meaningless to me.

My life is all about one thing now. One person.

Ripley.

She is the one thing that truly makes me happy. She is the one person who knows me totally and completely.

The only girl for me.

And now I've thrown her away. I've thrown away my one chance at love.

I've hurt her. I've hurt Ripley Sailor and I've run away from her like a coward. I couldn't face my problems, so instead, I hurt the one person I loved, and then I retreated into the shadows.

Ripley is the only person who truly cares for me, more

than even my family. My dad just thinks of me as a monetary commodity, a skilled surfer to bring in the sponsorship deals and the corporate donors. But Ripley is different. She actually cares if I get back on that surfboard, not because of money or sponsorships or brand deals, but simply because she knows it would be good for *me*.

Fuck. Surfing would be good for me. I just never saw it like that until Ripley forced me back on the board this morning.

This is enough.

Tide can go fuck itself.

I abruptly stand up, brushing the hands of the two girls who are basically hanging off on me off my body. My stoned dealer falls back into his seat, taken aback by my sudden movement. Stoned people don't like quick movements.

"Where are you going, dude?" he asks as I step over the VIP booth table and the numerous shot glasses and vodka bottles. The girls in the booth sit back to let me pass, pouting at my leaving. I'm the only reason they're here; the chance to sleep with the town's billionaire playboy lured them into Tide and to my VIP booth. Back in the times before Ripley, I would've gladly fulfilled their wishes.

But not anymore.

"None of your business," I reply to my dealer as I exit the booth and head straight to the nightclub's front door.

I am out of here.

Goodbye, Tide.

I am going to make things better.

27

COVE

THE SURFBOARD IS STILL EXACTLY where I had thrown it earlier by the beach cliffs. It lies there like an abandoned baby.

My baby.

The same board I learned to surf on when I was a teenager, thrown away exactly like I had thrown Ripley's emotions away. Sighing, I bend over and pick the surfboard up, brushing off the sand that's stuck to the fiberglass board.

I shouldn't have thrown you like that when you've been nothing but good to me. I'm sorry.

Carrying the surfboard under my arm, I stroll to the edge of the beach where the sand meets the raging ocean. The wet sand is cold against my toes. At the edge of the water, I take in a long deep breath, bringing in that fresh smell of both salt and sun deep into my lungs, and I survey the clear horizon. This secret beach is where some of the best moments of my life have happened. These last few weeks teaching Ripley to surf has healed my soul and has been, undoubtedly, the best thing to ever occur to me, and I've wrongly thrown it all away. I've wrongly thrown Ripley away.

Just like my board.

But now I am back to reclaim them.

I've been so lucky. So lucky to have Ripley in my life.

Those last few words I said to her painfully sting me. *Fuck off back to America.* I can't believe I told her that. Such cruelty to someone so pure.

Fuck. I've been such an asshole. I've thrown away the one person who truly loves me.

It's time to make it right.

I'd hoped, coming to the beach, that Ripley would still be here waiting for me.

She isn't.

Of course, she isn't.

She wasn't going to wait around for me, not after the way I treated her. My American girl is stronger than that.

She might be flying back right now, flying back because of me, flying back because I've been a world-class number one idiot.

She might already be in a plane right now, far above me heading home.

Fuck.

I take in one more deep breath of the ocean and then I reach into my pants, pulling out my phone. I find Ripley's name and call her.

The ringtone runs out. She hasn't picked up.

Yeah, she could be in the sky right now.

It could be too late.

Fuck, this is all your fault, Cove.

If I hadn't insulted her like that, if I hadn't freaked out in the shitty way I did, she'd still be here. I'd still be with her. But instead, I went crazy because of my own stupid insecurities and I threw her away like she means nothing to me.

But she means the world to you, doesn't she, Cove? And now she's gone, and it's all your fault.

There's only one way out of this, there's only one way to get her back - *if* she even wants to come back to me – and that'd be to own my stupid mistakes and prove myself to her. Prove how much she means to me. She might already be on a plane to America, but I'd still prove myself to her.

I have to.

I pick up my phone again, but this time, instead of calling her, I write out a short message.

That'll get her attention.

It's the only way. I have to prove myself.

Message sent, I throw my phone down in the sand, strip off my shirt so that I'm only in my board shorts, pick up my surfboard, and head directly into the ocean.

The freezing cold water doesn't affect me, and the roaring waves don't stop me as I walk out into the ocean. When it's too deep for me to continue, I jump on my surfboard, paddling even further out into the water. Further and further out. Further out into the ocean than I have any time with Ripley. I haven't been this far out in water since that fateful surf competition a year ago. I'm far out enough I can swim with wild dolphins.

I wait for the first big wave to come, any wave as long as it's tall enough to ride. I'm not patient at all; I need to do this *now*. I need to prove myself now. To myself. To Ripley.

I want Ripley to know that she's changed me, prove to her that she has made me a better man, that she has my heart completely and utterly in her hands. I want to prove to her I can do what she wants me to do and embrace my fears.

Be a surfer again.

Be *her* surfer boy.

I want her to know that.

The first wave comes, and I calmly accept it, pushing myself into the way of the wall of water. The wave picks me up with it and brings me to its foaming crest. I balance myself on the board, just like I'd done thousands of times before. I've done this thousands of times since I was a kid. This is completely natural to me.

I wait for the perfect moment to push myself up from the board.

And then I am standing.

Standing.

See? You can do this!

I'm finally proving it to myself, finally proving it to Ripley, that I really am a surfer, that I have nothing to fear. I just want her to see this. See that she's done this. In the last few weeks, she's given me hope. She's given me a reason to live again. All those months wasted over the past year feeling sorry for myself, it had to take Ripley from Queens to bring me out of my shell and embrace who I really am. I owe it all to her.

I am actually surfing!

But then pain ricochets down my scarred legs. Memories of all the surgeries fill my head in one violent burst. I can't hold myself up on the board anymore.

Fuck.

I lose my balance, then I feel myself flipping off.

No!

I am falling, falling back into the ocean. I lose all feeling.

And everything goes dark.

28

RIPLEY

It's a long drive to New Water Airport. A long-ass drive. I lie back in the reclined passenger seat next to Sandy and close my eyes, listening to the relaxing clicks of the car's indicators and the sound of Sandy's hands smoothly spinning over the steering wheel as we drive to the airport. My best friend hasn't turned the radio on, and I haven't asked her to, so we sit in silence as she drives the car through the town I've called home for the last few weeks and up past the ocean towards the airport. I prefer the silence.

Yeah, it is a long drive to the airport.

I just want to get out of here. I just want to leave. There are too many good memories here in this small town, memories that have turned bad. Rotten. Memories of Cove and me.

All those memories are false. I was living a lie.

Cove didn't really love me. He had run away. I was just another girl with a willing pussy to massage his ego for a few weeks, that's all. He told me to fuck off back to America when he'd grown tired of me. He didn't truly want me in his life.

I was just another one of his girls in the revolving doorway to his bed. Silly me for thinking I was special in any way.

It's time to go back home.

I'll just have to find - fund - my own way through university, make my own money somehow, support Mom somehow. I don't want to think about it. I will have to figure it all out, but right now, as I leave New Water, I just want to see my Mom again. Screw the worries and stress I'll have tomorrow. Now I just want to go home.

"I'm so sorry," I say softly to Sandy in her car. "I'm so sorry for everything."

"Stop repeating that," she replies sternly, eyes on the road.

"But I do. I *am*."

"Ripley, you don't have to be sorry for anything. In some ways it was my fault. I knew exactly what I was doing pairing you two together. I knew what a dick my brother was. I shouldn't have put you under that kind of stress."

"I'm sorry I couldn't help him. I know you really wanted me to. I know I was your last resort."

Sandy shakes her head. "If Cove couldn't change for you, then he won't change for anyone. He really is a lost cause now."

There's a lump in my throat as my emotions start to get the better of me. All the memories flood back into my mind. Cove and me on the beach. Our secret kisses. His tender touch on my body. His smile. "I really thought I loved him, Sandy. I really did."

She leans over and rubs my shoulder as tears well in my eyes. "I know, Ripley," she coos. "Men, hey?"

I laugh at the roll of her eyes. "Yeah, *men*."

"I just wish you were leaving under better circumstances. I'm really going to miss you, Ripley."

"You're always invited to New York, you know. Anytime."

"Well, I might just have to come, then," Sandy says, smiling at me. "I've always wanted to see the Big Apple. I'll just need to get the time off from the school."

"I hope you do. I could show you around like you've shown me around New Water."

"That would be magical."

Sandy takes her arm off me and turns back to her driving. I lean back against the car seat and stare out the window. We're passing up into the hills overlooking the ocean. The same road I had seen the dolphins on that first morning I arrived in Australia. I peer down through the window, hoping to catch another glimpse of the animals. Out in the waves I see the usual surfers, but no dolphins. The sun streams down on the water. It's a clear blue.

I am going to miss this.

I'm going to miss Australia and New Water, I'm going to miss Sandy, but, most of all, I'm going to miss the Cove I've fallen in love with.

The Cove that didn't really exist.

The fantasy Cove who was mine for a few glorious weeks.

The best few weeks of my life.

I sigh and close my eyes.

Goodbye, Australia.

My phone vibrates in my jeans pocket. A message. Who'd be doing that? This is my Australian number and I barely have any contacts in it.

I pull it out.

Cove.

I gasp and my heart trembles at his name.

Cove's messaged me?

I unlock my phone and, in a panic, open the message from him, my hand shaking as my fingers fumble with the screen.

My heart catches in my throat when I read it.

You're my dolphin, Ripley.

That was it. That's all it says.

But it makes everything change.

Cove?

I immediately know what he means.

My dolphin.

"Turn around," I say urgently to Sandy as soon as I read the message. "Turn the car around."

"What?"

I don't hesitate. "Turn around right now, Sandy. We need to go back."

She blinks at me, unresponsive. Confused.

"Forget about the airport," I say. "We need to turn around right now."

"Oh, okay."

"Before it's too late."

We do a U-turn to the other side of the road and I guide Sandy back down the highway, away from the town and towards the ocean instead.

Towards Cove and my secret beach.

She follows my directions as I take her down winding roads to the outskirts of the bush.

I know where we are going; I've done this so many times with Cove.

"What's wrong?" Sandy asks quietly as we reach the place where Cove and I would always park by the side of the trees. The same place he would always offer his hand. "Why have we turned around, Ripley?"

I look down at my phone, at the message Cove had sent

to me, then back up to Sandy. "We've turned around because Cove's doing something stupid. And I have to save him."

29

RIPLEY

I SEE THE SURFBOARD.

But no Cove.

I carry on rushing, sprinting over the sand, rushing across the beach towards the water.

Where's Cove? Where is he?

My head's scrambled as I frantically search with my eyes over the surf. No sign of him.

Where is he?

I reach the water's edge. No sign of him anywhere.

His surfboard's stuck on the wet sand, dragged into the shore by the crashing waves.

No, no, no.

That means only one thing.

Cove is still in the water.

Fuck.

There is only one thing I can do. I sprint into the water, still wearing my jeans and shirt. I awkwardly throw off my trainers as I ran; there is no time to slow down.

I think Sandy's behind me. I don't know. I hope she is, but I won't slow down to check behind.

Adrenaline flows through my veins. I don't have much time to find Cove.

I know what he'd done as soon as he messaged me in the car.

You're my dolphin, Ripley.

I knew then what he'd done, that he'd tried surfing again. Deep down he really was my Cove, and he'd wanted to prove it. I knew he'd try to surf alone at our secret beach.

But he is in no fit state to surf. His body - his *legs* - can't take it.

I have to help him.

And now, here I am, in the shallows of our secret beach, searching the water desperately for him.

For his body.

But I can't see it anywhere.

I don't want to think about his lifeless body, but there's every chance I will find it.

I don't want to think the worst.

"Cove!" I call out his name repeatedly until my throat becomes hoarse, but there's no response from the waves, no cry out in the ocean from his rough accent that I love, no sign of his cheeky smile. He is nowhere to be found in the water.

I keep looking.

There!

I see a body floating in the water.

Floating face down.

His dolphin tattoo is like a beacon to me.

Yeah, it's him.

"Cove!" I hear Sandy scream out from the shore behind me as I rush over to him.

I tip his body over so that his mouth is safely out of the

water, his bleach blonde hair sticking to his face. His eyes are closed.

I feel no pulse.

He isn't breathing.

Oh, please God, no.

With all my strength, I take a hold of his six-foot-tall body and drag him through the surf towards the sand. He's heavy, but I am determined. His body's limp, but I am strong.

I have to be strong for him.

Sandy rushes in and helps me pull him out of the water and onto the wet sand.

I check his pulse again. Still nothing.

Please, please, please.

He is so still, so silent, and I am so scared.

Please, please, please.

I know what I have to do. I remember my nursing text-books and the CPR section. All the notes I've made and all the pages I've read.

I want to be a nurse, and this is my chance to prove it.

I lay my hands upon his chest and start doing compressions, just like the textbooks say to do. I follow what I've learned.

This is Cove's only chance. We're miles away from the nearest hospital on a secluded beach with no path to get to.

I am his only chance of staying alive.

It all comes down to me.

My CPR skills are the only way to keep Cove alive, to bring him back to me.

I keep up the compressions as Sandy leans over. She calls out his name as I continue with CPR.

I'm going to do this. Don't give in, Cove. Don't give in.

"Stay with me," I whisper.

And then he's coughing. He is brought back to life so

quickly I nearly fall over in shock. He wakes up with a bang, saltwater spewing out his mouth. He coughs again, blinking open his eyes.

He's alive.

His blue eyes find mine.

He looks at me and only me. A shiver runs down my body.

Cove's back.

He really is alive.

"Hi," he says, his voice weak.

"Hello," is all I can respond with. I can't believe it. I'd thought he was gone. But he's here, he's alive.

"Hi, sis," he says, spotting Sandy over my shoulder. "Nice for you two to drop by."

"Hey."

"You alright?" I ask him. His chest rises and falls, his breathing returning to normal.

He slowly smiles. The old Cove I knew was coming back. "Never better," he replies.

Typical. Nearly dead and he makes a joke of the situation. Such a dick.

I laugh. Even though he's annoying the *hell* out of me, it's good to see him okay. He's going to be alright. "You nearly drowned! What the fuck were you doing? Why were you out here on your own?"

"I just thought I'd go for a little surf in the ocean, that's all."

"You stupid man," Sandy says from behind my shoulder, rolling her eyes. "I've got a total idiot for a brother."

Her idiot brother casually shrugs, still trying to breathe correctly.

I only have one question for him.

"I got your message... you weren't doing this for me, were you?"

Cove winks. "Don't be silly. I didn't do this for you." He attempts to push himself to a sitting position, but his arms are too weak. He collapses back into the sand. Sandy and I quickly rush to help, pulling him up together, and Cove grunts as our arms forced his body up. "Well, maybe I *did* do this for you."

"You did?"

"I think I wanted to prove something to you."

"By nearly drowning?"

"Look, I didn't think it through enough."

"That's putting it lightly."

"I think what I was trying to do - trying to *say* - is that I'm sorry. For everything."

"Oh, *Cove.*"

"Today – earlier – when I ran away, I didn't mean those words. I'm sorry for what I said. I really didn't mean those words. I was angry at myself for not being good enough for you. But instead of dealing with it, I lashed out at you. I lashed out at the one person who actually cares for me, and I am so sorry."

Oh, Cove.

My heart bleeds for him.

I wave him away. "Don't be sorry, Cove."

"I am, though. I was a dick and... I'm sorry. I did this stupid thing because I wanted to prove to you that I could stand up on the surfboard, that you've been good for me. That's why I did it."

"Well, it was a pretty stupid thing to do."

"It didn't really work, did it?"

"The sentiment's there, although there were easier and less risky ways to get my attention."

Of course, Cove picked the most dangerous.

"You had to pull me out of the water yet again. All I wanted to prove was how much you've changed me for the better these last few weeks," Cove says softly, his voice breaking. I just want to hold him tight against me and never let go, but he's not finished yet. "I wanted to prove to you that I love you."

What? What did he just say?

"You love me?" I ask, breathless.

It's like the whole world disappears from around my vision, leaving only Cove and I and the words he's whispering to me.

I love you.

He actually said it. A truth we both know, but we've been avoiding. A truth we've known since the first day we spent together.

But now he's actually said it.

"Yeah," he replies, smiling his gorgeous smile. "Yeah, I do. I love you, Ripley."

I lean in. Our faces are so close. "I love you, Cove."

Cove turns to Sandy. "Is that alright, sis? Are we breaking the deal?"

Sandy laughs. "Fuck that deal," she replies. "This is love."

Yeah, fuck it.

Cove winks at her and turns back to me, staring at me with a serious expression that I've rarely seen from him in all our time together. It's a look of complete sincerity. "I want to make this right, Ripley," he says. "I want to get back into surfing. You've made me realize that. You did. I couldn't do it without you. I've realized I can't do *anything* without you. I want to get back into surfing and I want your help."

"My help?"

"You've made me a better person, Ripley. You've made me a better man in every way, and it's only taken now, to when I nearly lost you, to realize that. I want to get back into surfing, but I need your help. I want you with me every step of the way. What do you say?"

He wants me to stay? He wants me to help him?

"Is that what you really want?" I ask.

His clear blue eyes stare deep into my own and I see how serious he is. I see how much he loves me. It's all true. Everything he's saying is true. He really wasn't like my dad after all. *Cove really does love me.*

"Yes," he replies. "That's what I really want."

He's my surfer boy.

I nod, turning to Sandy. She smiles back at me, standing a few yards away to give us space.

I think back on that first time we met, back when Cove stood naked outside his bedroom door. I think about the first day we spent together properly, and the way Cove tenderly taught me to surf. I think about the last few weeks, and how we've barely been apart.

The best weeks of my life.

If this isn't love, then nothing is.

Love is a mysterious force. You never know when or where it'll cross your path in life. And, when you least expect it, love finds you.

Love has found me now.

Cove and I have found each other.

Cove didn't think he deserved love, but he does.

He deserves my love.

Love can force you to see beyond the shallow façade someone's built up around themselves.

And I can see beyond Cove's façade.

I can see into his soul.

He loves me.

And I love him.

I've just got to let love in.

I turn back to Cove. "Okay, I'll help you," I say. "But I

just want you to promise me something. Something important."

"What?"

"So, you're not going to promise me?"

He cheekily smiles again. "I'm not promising anything until you tell me what it is, Ripley."

I lean in closer so that our faces nearly touch. "Promise me you'll lay off the drinks and the drugs and the girls. Can you do that?"

"What?" Cove asks with mock indignation. "*Every* girl?"

"Well," I reply with my own smile. "Every girl except one."

Cove faces Sandy. She nods at him. *Affirmation.* He faces back to me. "I promise," he says. He's telling the truth, I know. My heart begins to beat faster. His voice returns. He's back to his usual self.

"Yeah?"

"Yeah. Trust me."

30

FIVE MONTHS LATER

RIPLEY

Lying next to me, Cove stirs. He wakes.

"Hey," he says to me sleepily. He's so cute when he's in bed like this. He's like my own six-foot long hot water bottle.

"Hello."

He winks at me and closes his eyes again, relaxed. I smile and snuggle in closer against his warm, strong, muscular body as he wraps his big arm around me and pulls me in tight. I feel so protected in his solid embrace.

We're in Cove's giant bed together. We've done nothing all morning except fuck each other's brains out, and it was *glorious*. Cove can really use his tongue and I can really use my hips. We were both exhausted after our morning session, so we've decided to lie here, gently napping, into the sunny afternoon. There is nothing to do, no commitments for the rest of the day. Just him and me together in his giant silk bed.

And I love it.

We're in love.

But not all good things last forever. Our six months together are nearly up, and it is nearly time for me to head home. We've faithfully stuck to the deal we made to Sandy and their dad. Cove has been off drugs and alcohol since that day he tried to stand up again on the surfboard. He's been clean for five months. Five months spent with me every day. Five months growing more and more in love.

It's been good that Sandy and their dad had changed the terms of the deal to keep me. They didn't mind the fact that Cove and I are together. I mean, anyone can see we are, somehow, the perfect match, despite our differences. Anyone can see how much we've both helped and supported each other. I got him off drugs and booze and Cove's taught me to surf and to become an honorary Australian. Not too bad of a deal, if I must say so myself.

But now it's time for me to leave.

I want to stay. I want to be with Cove, no matter where we are.

But it's difficult.

My Mom is still back in New York. At least now the Finn family will support me through nursing university, at least now my Mom will never have to work another day of her life. But I just wish I can somehow still be with Cove even when I fly home.

Just a few years at university back home, that's all. Just make it through a few years and then I'll be with Cove again.

But, lying here in his bed up against him, my heart collapses at the thought. A few years is a long time to spend apart. It stretches out before me like an eternity. A few years in two different countries on the other side of the world. Apart. Alone.

I know I won't be able to bear it.

Cove stirs once again and opens his eyes. We look at each other for a long moment, soaking in each other's beautiful glare. His gorgeous blue eyes melt me under his gaze.

"Hey," he says again softly.

Yeah, he's so goddamn pretty.

"Hello."

Cove pulls back his arm around me and makes a move to the side of the bed.

"Where are you going?" I ask, pouting that his warm body has left my side so quickly.

What's he doing?

Cove smirks at me as he climbs out of bed. "I'm just going to get something."

He is fully naked as he jumps out of bed. Completely exposed, just as he'd been when I first met him that strange morning half a year ago.

Back then, it seemed like he was an asshole.

But that was a different Cove.

He's completely changed himself since then.

"Hey," I call out after him. He stops as I lean over the bed. I find what I'm looking for. *His pants.* I throw them at him, and Cove catches them in his hands. "Maybe put these on *before* you walk out there this time."

Cove smiles again at me. "Maybe I should."

He slips his pants over his legs and disappears out the bedroom door into the living room of Sandy's house.

I lean back into Cove's soft bed, snuggling up against the warm patch where his body has heated up.

This is too nice. I've got to remember this perfect

moment now before I forget it over the next few years when I'm back in cold, old New York.

The last few months have been nothing but pure magic. Cove has started to surf again, slowly at first, under my watchful eye. We've hired his old surfing coach from when he was a teenager to teach him again, and Cove has picked it up like a pro. He really is a natural in the water. In just a few short months, he's nearly regained his old abilities. One more year of this and he'll be back to where he was before the accident, if not even better. He might even be able to compete again. That would be something.

And he's told me he's doing all this for me.

Yeah, we really are in love.

The bedroom door slowly opens and in walks Cove. He's holding two glasses in his hands.

Glasses full of chocolate milkshake.

"Cove!"

"I thought I'd make your favorite," he says slyly. He brings the milkshakes to the side of the bed and hands one of the glasses over to me. I take it happily and gulp it down. I know I'll develop a milk mustache over my lips, but I don't care.

"This is so good," I say, pointing at the milkshake.

Cove reaches over and wipes my milk mustache off with his finger seductively. I giggle and he laughs.

"I thought you'd like it."

"Of course I would," I reply. I grab his face with my hands and pull him in for a long and deep kiss. "Thank you."

"So," Cove says. "I've been thinking."

"Oh, thinking? Don't do it too hard, otherwise you'll hurt your head."

"Very funny. You're such a joker," Cove replies. "Well, I've been thinking."

"Thinking about what?"

Cove smiles. "Thinking about a lot of things," he says. "And now I have an idea."

31

ONE YEAR LATER

RIPLEY

I RAISE the binoculars up to my eyes to get a better look at Cove. I spot him easily, a little black dot in the clear blue water. He's out there, far out there in the ocean, readying his surfboard. Waiting for the next good wave.

I watch him through the binoculars as he flicks his bleach blonde hair back in the sexy way he always likes to do it. He turns back over his shoulder to scan the horizon, looking for the next wave.

He's so damn sexy.

It won't be long before a good wave finds him.

It's his chance to win the Oceania Surf Competition.

That's where we are, his family and I, at the observation stand of the Oceania Surf Competition.

And Cove is only minutes away from winning it.

If only he is successful on this next wave.

If only he doesn't fall.

My heart's in my mouth as I watch him ready himself far out in the water, but Cove doesn't seem fazed at all. He's been practicing for this moment for nearly a year. And I should know, I've been with him every step of the way. This whole year of training for long hours every day has finally led to this moment, and I've been there right alongside him every single day.

I hope he doesn't fall. I hope he wins.

But even if he does fall off his board, and even if he does somehow fail the competition, I won't love him any less. I'll still be beside him, no matter what happens. He's my surfer boy, and I'm his American girl. We stick together no matter what.

Still, it *will* be pretty nice if he does win.

"Can you see him?" my Mom asks. She's next to me, clutching the railings of the observation stand. She's seemingly more nervous than I am, and that's saying something. "Is he okay?"

"Yeah," I reply, smiling. "He's out there. He looks like he's got a handle on things."

"That's good."

I'm so happy my Mom's here. It hasn't been easy getting her over to Australia. Ripley's dad has had to muscle in on his mates in border control to process the tricky visa. He's also had to do the same with my own visa so that I can stay in the country indefinitely.

This last year has brought about major changes. Changes to everything.

Cove's idea - back in his bedroom exactly a year ago - was for me to study nursing in Australia instead of flying back home.

He thought I should study at New Water's state-of-the-art hospital. That way we could still be together. He could continue his surfing training and I could start my nursing training without spending any time apart. Win-win.

And what a good idea it was.

The only problem was my Mom. But, for a billionaire family like the Finns, that was no *real* problem. Thanks to Cove's Dad we were both able to secure Australian visas and be able to stay here indefinitely. Mom was more than happy to come; Australia was a far better retirement lifestyle than a cramped New York apartment. She loves New Water. She loves the beach, and she loves the fresh seafood on offer every day. Not too bad for a nurse from Queens to end up in a paradise like this.

"Here you go, Mrs. Sailor." It's Sandy, bringing over three coffees she's gone to get from the vendor for Mom and me. My Mom thanks her as I take the steaming takeaway cup from Sandy and hand her my binoculars. Sandy peers through them at Cove waiting on his surfboard far out in the ocean. "I don't want to jinx it, but he looks good out there."

"He sure does," I reply, raising the hot coffee to my mouth.

Out of the corner of my eye, I see Sandy's dad walking over to join us. He's been talking to a group of high-flying corporate sponsors in the VIP box, presumably over a deal to do with Cove. Even if my boyfriend doesn't win today, he's still all set for a professional career. My boy's too skilled a surfer for industry bigwigs to let go to waste, so he'll be lapped up by some sponsorship company before today is out. His career is basically a guaranteed success.

I feel a twang of pride for Cove. He's struggled so much in the last year to get to where he is today.

It just goes to prove that hard work really can help you succeed in anything.

"Hello, Ripley. Hello, Mrs. Sailor," Michael Finn greets Mom and me as he approaches us. He turns to look out at the black dot of Cove paddling in the ocean. "He's been doing well today."

"He has been," my Mom agrees, nodding.

Cove's dad turns to me and puts his hand on my shoulder. "He's doing so well today because of you, Ripley. I want to congratulate you on everything you've done for this family."

I blush. "It wasn't me, Mr. Finn. It was all Cove."

"Well," Sandy says, butting in. "The only reason he's got anything done was because he was chasing you."

I laugh and continue to sip on my coffee.

The PA system announces Cove over the loudspeaker. He's gearing up to take on a wave. We all rush to the front of the railings to get a better look at him. Sandy hands me my binoculars back and I peek through them at Cove on his surfboard.

A big wave's coming, and he's getting ready to paddle onto it.

A big fucking wave.

This is his chance. His chance to win.

And he takes it.

Cove paddles into the path of the wave and takes it. His board, and him, shoot down the side of it. Within moments, he's standing.

He's going to win.

Cove surfs the wave into shore.

It's perfect. Perfectly done. Perfect scores.

I can't help but jump up and down in joy.

Cove has won.

* * *

"First place goes to Cove Finn!"

The crowd goes wild. Everyone knows about his reputation, about his past, about his fall from the surfboard just a few years ago. But now Cove Finn had returned, triumphantly, back to Oceania Surf Competition. And he has *won*.

I watch on with pure delight as Cove lifts the massive gold trophy above his head on the stage. He beams out to the crowd.

I know he can't see me, that I'm just a speck in the corner of the crowd, but my pride for him doesn't dim.

I turn to my Mom and she smiles at me.

Everything's worked out. Everything's perfect. And now I just want to see my surfer boy and be with him.

Cove bounces off the stage, a mob of reporters and corporate sponsors surrounding him; a gaggling crowd that swamps him in one big push. I can't see Cove through the mass of people scrambling for his attention. I'm stuck in the back of the crowd, looking on, hoping for a glimpse of my surfer boy. But he's gone, surrounded by the vultures braying for his attention.

Oh well, he does need to talk to all the important people. I'll just wait for him until he's finished. No problem.

But then I see him.

Cove's ignoring everyone. He is walking straight through the crowd, not bothering to talk to any of the important people. He isn't giving any of his attention to the corporate sponsors or the journalists or even the famous surfers who want a word.

Instead, he is heading straight for me.

Cove, holding that massive golden trophy he's just won, walks straight up to me and whispers in my ear as I stand frozen to the spot.

He's whispering in my ear.

"You did this," he says slowly. "And it was all down to

you and me. A dream team, so how about we stay that team forever?"

My heart stops.

"What are you saying?"

"I'm saying will you marry me, my *American girl*?"

I don't even have to think about it.

I immediately whisper back, "yes, my *surfer boy*."

I will marry him.

WANT to find out about Sandy's own love story?

Go to rebeccacastle.com to find the links for The Teacher (Surfer Town #2)

ABOUT THE AUTHOR

Rebecca has had the storytelling bug since... forever!

What Rebecca likes most is writing steamy hot filthy romances with sweet happy endings sprinkled with some delicious bad boys.

Born and raised in an Aussie coastal town, she loves travelling around the world - meeting new people and discovering their stories.

Aside from adventuring she also enjoys a good rainy day in with a good book or at a hot beach catching the sun.

She's a world-class napping professional. You'll most likely find her asleep snuggled up on a sofa somewhere cozy.

For other titles and information please visit
rebeccacastle.com

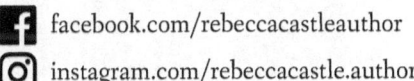 facebook.com/rebeccacastleauthor
instagram.com/rebeccacastle.author